# DIMSIE MOVES UP

It's the summer term at Jane's – or the Jane Willard Foundation, to give the school its proper name. To their surprise, Dimsie and four of her friends are moved up a form – but Rosamund, Dimsie's closest friend, is left behind in the Third Form. Already known for her initiative (or 'cheek', as the older girls call it!) Dimsie takes steps to remedy this unsatisfactory situation. In the process Dimsie finds herself crossing swords with the mischief making Nita, becoming a founder member of the Anti-Soppists Society, rescuing the head girl, exploring a smuggler's cave – and, in a final thrilling chapter, ends up in real danger of losing her life.

BY THE SAME AUTHOR
AND
IN THE SAME SERIES

*Dimsie Goes to School*

# DIMSIE MOVES UP

## DORITA FAIRLIE BRUCE

JOHN GOODCHILD PUBLISHERS
WENDOVER

John Goodchild Publishers,
70 Carrington Crescent,
Wendover,
Buckinghamshire
HP22 6AN

*First published in this revised edition 1983*
© Copyright Dorita Fairlie Bruce's Executors 1983

British Library Cataloguing in Publication Data
  Bruce, Dorita Fairlie
  Dimsie moves up.
  I. Title
  823'.914[J]      PZ7

ISBN 0-903445-66-2

Edited by Judith Hayter
Cover and text design by Jim Wire
Cover illustration by Gordon King

Set in 11 on 13 pt Baskerville by John Buckle (Printers) Limited,
Great Yarmouth, and printed and bound by Woolnough Bookbinders
Limited, Wellingborough.

# CONTENTS

# CHAPTER 1

# PROMOTION

The private bus from Westover drew up with a crunching of gravel and jarring of brakes before the pillared portico of the Jane Willard Foundation, and out scrambled schoolgirls, big and small, a merry, laughing crowd, to be seized upon and borne off by friends who had already arrived.

"Erica! Is Erica Innes there? And Dimsie Maitland?" called an excited junior, hopping on the steps on one foot, while she held the other in her hand. "Oh, there you are! Come in quickly! I've got some absolutely thrilling news! I've simply got to tell you before you report to Miss Yorke."

"Hurry up, then," ordered Erica Innes, a slim girl of twelve, with straight, dark hair and a fringe. "How long have you been back, Mabs? An hour? Trust you! No one else could have managed to collect any news in that time."

"I don't suppose so," said Mabs Hunter modestly. "I believe it's a gift. I'm not musical and I can't draw, but I do know what's going on. Meg Flynn says I'll make a jolly good journalist some day."

"Well, but what's the news?" interposed Dimsie impatiently. "We shall have to go into the drawing-room in a minute."

"Not yet – there are loads of people to go first, and the seniors always – oh, all right, then! I'll tell you. We've been moved up; we're in the Lower Fourth now!"

"What? All of us?"

"Well, you two, and Pam, and Jean, and me. Isn't it a laugh?"

"I can hardly believe they'd move half the form up whole-

1

sale like that, and at the beginning of the summer term," said Erica sceptically.

"Honest – ask Pamela Hughes if you don't believe me. There she is. She came by the same bus as I did."

At that moment Pamela caught sight of them, and came running across the big hall to greet the new arrivals.

"Hi, everyone! Did you have nice holidays?" she cried. "I had an absolutely super time. I rode a cow bare-back round the field till she chucked me. No – I fell soft, but Mother was rather surprised I wasn't killed."

"Gosh, I never thought of trying that," said Dimsie regretfully. "Pam, is it true that we're all in the Lower Fourth now? Mabs says so."

"Yes – honestly! Miss Yorke told us herself. She said Miss Yelland had been very pleased with our work, and we'd done well in the exams last term; but I believe it's because a whole lot of new kids have come who couldn't go anywhere but into the Third Form, so they've moved us up to get rid of us and make room."

"I wonder what it'll be like," said Erica dubiously. "Betty Grey and Joan Hardy and that set are sure to try and boss us. Are we still in the junior dormitory?"

"No," answered Mabs. "We're in Room 10; you know – the room looking out to the front, opposite the head of the stairs."

"But," objected Dimsie, "there are only five beds in that dormitory."

"I know. We four are there, but I can't tell you whether Rosamund Garth or Jean Gordon has got the fifth, because neither of them has come yet. It's hard luck on the one who's left behind with the new kids."

"Dimsie and Erica! No hanging about there," said one of the older girls reprovingly. "You ought to be in the drawing-room reporting yourselves."

The two juniors obediently disappeared through the drawing-room door, to be greeted by the headmistress, a slim, brown-eyed woman with unruly dark hair and a wonderfully kind smile, which sinners knew from experience could fade into sternness when necessary. She spoke to them for a few minutes about their holidays and the coming term, and then turned to welcome a late-comer. Finding themselves dismissed, the two juniors raced upstairs to inspect their new quarters and unpack their belongings, while Pamela and Mabs, having already done so, balanced themselves on the bed-rails in preference to more comfortable seats, and discussed adventures, past and future.

"This is very nice, of course," said Dimsie, looking about her pensively at the cheerful bedspreads and hangings, "and I like the parrots on the cubicle curtains, but I've slept in the junior dormitory ever since I came to Jane's, and it's rather a wrench to leave it."

"Nonsense!" retorted Erica briskly, as she crammed underclothing into a drawer with more regard for speed than order. "You had to leave it some time. You couldn't go on sleeping there till you were about ninety and a prefect, so you may as well change now as later on. You know that quotation out of Shakespeare that Sylvia Drummond put in her prize essay last term? It struck me very much at the time when Miss Yorke read it out to us, but I can't quite recall it for the moment."

"'Tis better to have loved and lost than never to have loved at all'?" suggested Pam, but Erica shook her head.

"No, stupid! That's Wordsworth. Something about the old order changing . . . Never mind, I'll ask Sylvia tomorrow. Anyhow, you see what I mean, don't you, Dimsie?"

Dimsie, who was kneeling on the floor in front of the chest of drawers she was to share with Pamela, sat back on her heels and pondered.

"I don't think I do," she admitted candidly.

"Don't bother to explain any more, Eric," interposed Mabs hurriedly. "I, for one, am very glad we've been shifted, anyhow."

"Why?" queried Pam with interest. "Were you tired of the junior dormitory?"

Mabs shook her head mysteriously, and her brown cork-screw curls bobbed up and down like springs.

"Not exactly, but I had reasons for wishing to be moved."

"She means the mouse behind the wardrobe," declared Erica scornfully. "You know how it scared her last term. Mabs

3

always likes to make a mystery of the simplest things."

"I don't!" cried Mabs indignantly. "At least, not the simplest things, but when I know something frightfully interesting I like to make you guess it if you can. And it wasn't that old mouse, so there!"

"Well, what was it then?" demanded Erica impatiently. "Listen, Mabs, am I monitress of this bedroom, or are . . ." Her voice died away suddenly, and she looked rather foolish.

"That's just what nobody knows yet," returned Mabs triumphantly, "seeing the monitress list for the term hasn't been posted. So you needn't start bullying us quite so early, Eric!"

"But of course she will be monitress," said Dimsie, "seeing she's the eldest and always has been – monitress of our lot, I mean. Do stop arguing, Mabs, and tell us why you wanted to move."

"Because of something somebody told me – oh, all right, then! It was Margaret, my sister. When she first came to Jane's there was a prefect whose grandfather had stayed here years ago when it belonged to Jane Willard's parents, and he said there was a secret passage connected with one of the bedrooms."

"What?" cried Dimsie and Pamela in unison.

"There might be," mused Erica. "It's an awfully old house, you know."

"And ever since she told me," proceeded Mabs, "I've been dying to sleep in all the dormitories till I found the right one and could explore the secret passage."

"We might have a look now," suggested Pam, ripe, as usual, for any adventure; but before the idea could be taken up they were interrupted by a sniffing sound outside the door, and in burst the two remaining members of their crowd: Jean Gordon, a small, dark Scottish girl, rather like a robin redbreast, and golden-haired Rosamund Garth, with her big blue eyes swimming in tears.

"Oh, there you are!" cried Mabs, disregarding the signs of woe, which were frequent with Rosamund and meant very little as a rule. "Do tell us – which of you is sleeping here?"

Rosamund choked, and Jean patted her on the back with

kindly concern.

"I am," she answered, "but it's frightfully hard luck on poor Rosamund. Yes, she really has got something to cry about this time, I'm afraid. Not only is she left behind in the junior dormitory, but she hasn't been moved up with the rest of us – she's still in the Third Form!"

Rosamund's friends were full of sympathy at once, and Dimsie, springing up, flung her arm round the afflicted damsel's heaving shoulders.

"Poor thing! What horrible luck! Never mind – must be a mistake, and we'll soon put it straight. You'll find you've been moved up all right, and – and – of course, there isn't room for five of us in here, but I'll go and ask Miss Yorke to let me stay behind in the old room instead of you."

"Oh, no, Dimsie!" wailed Rosamund. "I couldn't let you. And besides, there isn't any mistake, and it won't be put straight. That sickening Miss Yelland said I hadn't worked nearly as hard as the rest of you, and that she couldn't think of moving me up a form. She – she might have stopped to think, though, before blackening my name to the headmistress. And we've always been together before, and I shall be left with a lot of new kids and dull old ones, and I'll probably . . ."

"Listen," said Dimsie, giving her a little shake. "I've got a plan! No – really! But you must stop crying at once. I can't do it now because she's busy with people arriving, but after supper I shall go to Miss Yorke, and I shall beg her to give you a chance, and you must come, too, and promise to work your very hardest. You know you can if you like, Rosamund."

"Well!" exclaimed Erica in a shocked voice, "I've always known you had a cheek, Dimsie Maitland, but I never thought the day would come when I'd see you advising Miss Yorke as to who should be moved up and who shouldn't. You'll certainly be expelled one of these days!"

"You've told me that before," returned Dimsie imperturbably, "and it hasn't happened yet. And you won't see me, 'cause you won't be there – only Rosamund and me."

"Not me!" retorted Rosamund ungratefully, as she dried her eyes. "Whoever else is there I shan't be! I never heard of anything so mad. You'll simply get yourself moved down again for cheek."

# CHAPTER 2

# A VAIN APPEAL

When Dimsie Maitland had made up her mind to a course of action it took more than the arguments of her school-fellows to dissuade her. Accordingly, though Rosamund firmly refused to go with her, she arrived alone, after supper, at the door of the headmistress's study, and knocked – not without a shiver of nervousness, though nothing would have induced her to confess it.

She had hoped to find Miss Yorke alone, but in this she was doomed to disappointment, for on the cushioned seat below the open window sat Sylvia Drummond, the headgirl, going through some lists which Miss Yorke herself, seated nearby in her low armchair, was hurriedly jotting down on loose sheets of paper.

"Come in, dear," said the headmistress, glancing round at the small figure in the doorway. "Just see if these are correct, Sylvia; I'll attend to them in a minute. Yes, Dimsie? Do you want to speak to me about anything?"

"Please, Miss Yorke, it's about Rosamund Garth," said Dimsie, closing the door behind her, and looking slightly scared at her own temerity. "If you don't mind very much, could she be in the Lower Fourth, too? You see, she's always been with the rest of us, and she simply hates being left behind with mostly new kids. It's so – so horrid for her!"

Her voice broke a little, and her big brown eyes had a very pleading look as she took a step nearer the headmistress's chair.

"Please!" she urged. "Rosamund's awfully miserable, even for her."

Sylvia Drummond looked up from her lists with poised

pencil, and raised her fine eyebrows comically, while the corners of Miss Yorke's firm mouth twitched a little.

"Come here, Dimsie," she said gently, and her warm eyes looked straight into Dimsie's. "I quite understand your distress on your friend's account, but I am afraid I can't do as you ask me – not just yet, at any rate. You see, Miss Yelland tells me that Rosamund hasn't been working as hard as the rest of you and she doesn't quite know whether she is equal to the same lessons. If that is the case, it wouldn't be kind to move her into a higher form, where the work would be more difficult still."

"But – but, Miss Yorke, Rosamund *can* do our work," Dimsie blurted out eagerly. "It's only because . . ."

She stopped abruptly, for she realized that she had been on the verge of giving her friend away, but Miss Yorke's eyes twinkled as she completed the sentence.

"Because she has been rather lazy sometimes, is that it? Well now, Dimsie, do you think it would be fair to the rest of you to move Rosamund up?"

Dimsie's eyes fell before the keen, quizzical glance, and she fiddled uncomfortably with the buttons of her blouse.

"No-o," she admitted, "I s'pose it wouldn't."

"Quite right," said Miss Yorke, "it would not. But I'll tell you what I might do, Dimsie – only it won't depend on me, you know. If Rosamund begins straightaway to work as hard as she can, and if Miss Yelland tells me that she is really trying to make up for lost time – then I might move her up at half-term, perhaps."

Dimsie's anxious face cleared. This did look like a compromise, after all, and her sense of justice told her that it was fair.

"Oh, thank you, Miss Yorke; thank you! Rosamund will work, really she will! But, please . . ."

"Well, what is it now?" asked Miss Yorke smiling.

The colour rushed over Dimsie's small face, and she hung her head a little.

"Please, you don't think it was terribly cheeky of me to ask you about it, do you? I thought it was the best plan, but the others were dreadfully shocked."

Miss Yorke laughed out loud and a half-suppressed chuckle broke from Sylvia on the window-seat.

"No, dear, I don't think it was at all cheeky. It's nearly always a good plan to come straight to headquarters if you have a grievance or a difficulty to be cleared up, and I am always ready to listen to you. Indeed, I sometimes wish you little girls would do so oftener. I am not such a very terrible person, after all, am I, Dimsie?"

Dimsie reddened again.

"I think you're an extremely kind person," she said earnestly. "If you weren't headmistress nobody would be a bit afraid of you – honestly! Please may I go and tell Rosamund now?"

"Yes – run along! And, remember, it's up to Rosamund what will happen at half-term."

"I'm afraid," observed Dimsie wisely to herself as she ran down the wide front staircase to the junior sitting-room, "I'm very much afraid it rests a lot more with me. Rosamund's so slapdash about her work, if someone doesn't keep her at it – and really, last term she hardly bothered at all."

Upstairs, Miss Yorke gathered her notes together and glanced across at Sylvia with a smile, which showed the mutual understanding between them. The headmistress of Jane's was on excellent terms with her girls, particularly Sylvia, the headgirl.

"I like that child's spirit," she observed, "and her delightful straightforwardness; her set among the juniors are all more or less imbued with the same sturdy honesty and lack of affectation. They'll do the Lower Fourth good."

"Yes," agreed Sylvia warmly. "They need it, too – feeble little wretches those Lower Fourth girls are! Forever hanging round the older girls, needing to be told what to do!"

Miss Yorke shrugged her shoulders.

"They're at that very trying stage," she said. "Now, what about Joyce Lamond for librarian this term, Sylvia? Let's get on with these lists."

The junior sitting-room was a large basement room with deep-silled windows raised four feet above the floor, and on one of these sills, with legs dangling, sat Dimsie's five friends anxiously awaiting her return.

"What ages you've been!" was Erica's greeting when at

length she reappeared. "We've had Rosamund almost in tears again because she was sure Miss Yorke had gobbled you up. It wouldn't have been more than you deserved, either!"

"Miss Yorke was extremely nice to me," declared Dimsie with dignity, looking up at them from below with her hands behind her back. "I asked her if she thought it was cheeky of me, and she said certainly not, and she only wished you'd all do the same."

"It's perfectly weird," declared Jean Gordon with grudging admiration, "how Dimsie gets praised for doing things which would get anyone else into an awful row. But what about Rosamund? Is she to be moved up with us after all?"

Dimsie shook her head regretfully.

"Not exactly – here, make room for me beside you – I did my best, Ros, you know, but Miss Yorke was a wee bit awkward about your lessons and what Miss Yelland had said. She's promised, though, that if you work hard till half-term she'll think it over then."

"Till half-term," echoed Rosamund dolefully. "Oh, Dimsie, that's such a long time to work hard! Six whole weeks!"

"It isn't so bad when you get into the way of it," said Erica encouragingly. "The first few days are always the worst, and after that you sort of become used to it."

"Anyhow, it's got to be done, Rosamund," said Dimsie decidedly. "Tell you what – I'll hear your prep every evening before we start playing records. Then you'll *have* to do your lessons, because you won't want to keep me too long hearing them – see?"

"But, Dimsie, it will be such a bore for you," faltered Rosamund.

"Not if you know them beforehand. You must see that it's much the best plan," argued Dimsie. "Hey! Here come Betty Grey and Joan Hardy. I wonder how they'll like having us in their form."

"Oh, that'll be all right," said Betty condescendingly, as she strolled up in time to overhear the last words. "We shan't mind so long as none of you start hanging round Miss Moffatt and getting in our way. After all, we've been in her form much longer than you lot."

"Whatever do you mean?" queried Jean bluntly, while the rest of the row on the window-sill stared at the pair below in round-eyed astonishment.

"Just what we say," reiterated Betty, the spokeswoman. "You mustn't go giving her flowers or sweets, or tidying her desk for her, or carrying her things: it wouldn't be fair to us."

"You must be nuts!" said Erica with conviction. "We shouldn't dream of doing such things. I'd like to see Miss Yelland if any of us meddled with her desk! You don't mean to say . . ."

"Shh, Eric!" interposed Mabs Hunter quickly. "I know all about it. Another Lower Fourth girl told me last term – I think it was Winnie Hatton – she said a lot of them were like that in the Fourth Form just now. It isn't only Miss Moffatt, either; some of them are always sucking up to the seniors – Meg Flynn or Daisy Milne, for example. And Winnie herself runs around for Mademoiselle."

"Mademoiselle!" The hoot of derision was hardly flattering to the dainty, but somewhat ineffective, little Frenchwoman who taught French at the Jane Willard Foundation.

"I asked Mother about it in the holidays," resumed Mabs. "She says it's a sort of complaint girls get, like measles. She thinks they all go through it in time."

"Well, we shan't!" said Erica with great decision. "Just remember, whether I'm to be monitress in our room or not, at least no one can prevent me from being the eldest, and I won't have that kind of rubbish! I know, we can start a secret society to fight against it! Rosamund had better join it, too, for she's just the sort of idiot to go giving people flowers and sitting next them, and if she's to be moved up at half-term she can't begin too soon. Rosamund's the only one of us I feel at all anxious about."

"You needn't," returned Rosamund placidly. "But of course I'll join. What's the society to be called, Erica?"

"I don't know," said Erica. "I shall have to think it over, and make some rules. You can't have a thing of that sort without rules, you know."

"I should have thought we'd got plenty already," said Pam Hughes disgustedly. "without you going and making any more."

"Nonsense!" answered Erica loftily. "You don't want to turn wet like Betty and Joan, do you? Well, you'll have to do as I tell you. Honestly, we've really got to stop this sort of soppiness."

# CHAPTER 3

# PRIMROSE GARTH'S TROUBLE

Sylvia Drummond, cool and elegant in her blue cotton dress, came slowly down the steps from the open french windows of the senior schoolroom, and paused on the gravelled terrace to look about her.

Just below were the tennis courts, every one of them occupied, for it was the second Saturday of the term, and the girls were all keen to begin practising for the various fixtures looming ahead. Sylvia's quick eyes scanned the courts, but, failing to find what they sought, she walked along to the end of the terrace and down a little path into the wood.

The wood at Jane's was a delightful place. Sheltered from the sea winds by the steep down in front, it clambered along the ridge on which the school stood, in clumps of larch and fir with grassy glades between, till it reached the valley. There, along the side of the playing fields, it became a screen of elms, horse-chestnuts and cedars.

"Is Primrose Garth down there?" asked Sylvia of a knot of juniors who were strolling upwards, their arms intertwined.

"Primrose Garth? I don't know. Did you see her, Jean? Rosamund, did you notice your sister down in the field?"

"No," said Rosamund, "but I think she's somewhere in the wood, Sylvia. I saw her go down the path with a book just after tea. Shall I shout?"

"No, thank you," said the headgirl hastily. "I'll find her for myself. What are you lot doing?"

"We're trying to find a good place to act in. There's no shade in the field."

"Oh – charades? I used to enjoy . . ."

"We're not playing charades," interrupted Erica rather crushingly. "We're going to do a play, and make up the words as we go along."

Sylvia shook her head as if in disapproval.

"That sort of thing is all very well in winter, though even then you might vary your games occasionally, but in the summer term you want to be out doing something more active, or you'll turn soppy."

"Oh, not soppy, Sylvia!" cried Erica in alarm. "That's the last thing we'll be! But what can we do? We can't play tennis when the courts are simply swarming with seniors."

"What about cricket, then? The elevens never go on to practise before six in the evening, and your prep is always done by four."

Erica fidgeted in silence, digging a pebble out of the mossy path with the toe of her sandal.

"Don't you like cricket?" demanded Sylvia in astonishment. "Some of you were keen enough last summer."

"It's all Nita Tomlinson's fault," burst out Jean Gordon, the outspoken. "Now that she's games-captain she says she won't have us messing up the pitch. And she says that we'll never play decently when we're older if we muck around now."

Sylvia frowned sharply, but the juniors were astute enough to know that her displeasure was not directed against them.

"I never suggested you should 'muck around'. Of course, Miss Yelland's time is taken up with coaching the elevens and the tennis teams, but you can perfectly well use the pitch if there's a prefect or senior of some sort in charge of you."

"We don't like to bother them," said Erica politely.

"Most of them wouldn't be bothered," added Jean.

The headgirl considered the question for a moment, then said briefly: "Never mind. Go and play anything you like just now. I'll see what can be done later on."

Erica, Jean, and Rosamund wandered on, and Sylvia, forsaking the path, plunged downwards through the young green bracken to continue her search for Primrose.

She soon found her, perched on the low branch of an old cedar, with a book in her lap which she was not reading and a troubled look on her face. Primrose was not as pretty as her younger sister, Rosamund, but she has the same appealing violet eyes and corn-coloured hair, and what her features lacked in regularity they made up for by showing a good deal more character than the fair Rosamund could at present lay claim to.

"Oh, there you are, lazybones!" exclaimed Sylvia, dropping among the dry brown needles which carpeted the ground below the tree. "Why aren't you up at the courts?"

"Why aren't *you?*"

"I've just been practising in the lower music-room, and afterwards I thought I'd come looking for you. Listen, Primrose, you're welcome to say if you think I've no right to barge into your affairs, but – is there trouble between you and Meg?"

Primrose did not reply for a moment. The book on her lap slipped down, falling with a soft thud to the ground, while she sat with loosely-clasped hands, staring into the cool shadows of the pink-tufted larches.

"You see," urged Sylvia gently, "I thought I might be able to help, but of course I don't know if you want anyone interfering."

"I don't think I do," replied Primrose slowly. "Thanks, all the same Sylvia. It's nice of you to offer, but – well, Meg and I have been friends ever since we came to Jane's, and – if she doesn't want me around any more, well, I can't exactly push in where I'm not wanted. What good would it do, anyhow?"

"Not much," admitted Sylvia, and picking up a cone she tossed it from hand to hand. "Still, there might be less crude ways of doing it."

Primrose shook her head.

"I simply don't want to butt in unless I'm invited," she said. "You'd be the same yourself, Sylvia, if it was a case of you and Daphne, you know."

Sylvia's keen grey eyes softened suddenly, but she was too tactful to voice her opinion as to the difference between Daphne Maitland's character and Meg Flynn's.

"I expect you're right," she murmured.

"It's all Nita Tomlinson's fault!" broke out Primrose bitterly, in the very words used by Jean Gordon half an hour earlier. "It's been going on ever since last Christmas term,

Sylvia, when you were away for so many weeks with that bad knee. Meg has never realized what's happening, but Nita has been trying to turn her against me. They are both good at games, you see, and I'm not much use at anything but cricket. Now they're going to partner each other for the tennis doubles, and they'll always be together."

"Yes," said Sylvia, "I saw them playing against Nell Anderson and Nancy just now."

"Don't think I'm such a twit as to want Meg to give up her tennis just because I'm not good enough to play with her," said Primrose earnestly. "It's not that. And, of course, I don't mind her being friends with Nita, though I don't much like the girl myself – I've never liked her since she hoodwinked us all into treating Daphne so badly over that gossip about her mother. But it seems to me, Sylvia, that if a girl is friends with Nita she has to drop everyone else, and that's exactly what Meg is doing."

Sylvia nodded gravely.

"Nita is such a jealous little cat – she can't bear to see anyone being friendly with anyone else. I wish Providence in the shape of her parents would see fit to remove her from our lives by sending her to some other school. Her latest piece of selfishness is trying to stop those wretched little juniors from playing cricket."

"How?"

Sylvia repeated her conversation with the three younger girls, and added, "I'm going to put a stop to that little scheme, though. It's bad for the kids to be doing nothing but play-acting all year round. It isn't sufficient exercise, and besides, they'll start getting affected. They must have their cricket like every-body else, and I'll have to make some arrangement about coaching them."

"I can do it three afternoons in the week, if that's any good to you," volunteered Primrose. "We could have the pitch from five to six, or do some practice at the nets."

"Thanks," said Sylvia, "that would be a tremendous help. I expect Daph would take them, one evening, and I could, too – oh, I'll work out a scheme easily. Nita won't like it, but that can't be helped."

"I'll try to see if I can get Meg to coach them a bit," said Primrose, speaking more hopefully. "After all, it's ridiculous if I can't ask her a little thing like that. We haven't quarrelled, or even disagreed."

"Of course not," returned Sylvia. "Only Nita is trying to get her to transfer her allegiance, and your pride won't let you put up a fight against Nita. That's the matter in a nutshell. Come up to the courts with me, and let's see if we can fit in a few games before supper. I expect there won't be such a crowd there now."

# CHAPTER 4

# THE ANTI-SOPPISTS

Next Monday, during morning school, a scrap of exercise paper circulated round the Lower Fourth. It bore a flaming cross crudely executed in red felt-tip, and underneath in sprawling characters was written, "The Council Chamber, 5 o'clock." Two-thirds of the form had no idea what it meant or who had started it, but the four girls newly moved up, who recognized the secret sign of Erica Innes, grinned and nodded to each other, and five o'clock found them hurrying down a secluded path in the shrubbery, led by Erica in person.

"I've decided about our league," she told them. "What it's to be called, rules and everything, and now we're going to the council chamber so as we can talk it over in peace."

A bend in the path and a break in the glossy-leaved laurel bushes showed them a dilapidated minibus drawn up in a green clearing. It had been bought and presented to the juniors of Jane's in a fit of benevolence by one of the school's trustees. Erica stopped abruptly and stared in disgust. Inside and out, scrambling all over the broken-down bus, in evident enjoyment of its battered charms, was a bevy of smaller girls – the "new kids" whose arrival at Jane's had, according to Pamela Hughes, been the cause of her own and her friends' promotion.

"They've found our council chamber! What cheek!" muttered Jean Gordon resentfully.

"After all," urged Mabs Hunter, "they're only Third Form infants, and new, besides. Can't we tell them to clear out?"

But Erica, though annoyed, prided herself on possessing a keen sense of justice.

"No. They've as good a right to be there as we have; but it's a proper nuisance, because I don't know where we can hold our councils now without being interrupted."

"I do, though," said Dimsie Maitland suddenly. "I know a better place than that, where no one else would ever think of going. Come on!"

She turned abruptly, and pushing her way between the bushes, led her little party round the side of the house and downwards into the least frequented part of the wood. Here, at the foot of the slope, stood an ancient tool shed, its door hanging on a broken hinge. Dimsie pushed it open and entered in triumph.

"There!" she said, waving her hand proudly. "Isn't it cosy? There are flowerpots to sit on, and plenty of light if we leave the door open."

"I must say, Dimsie," declared Erica approvingly, "you're rather good at having ideas. After all, we *were* getting rather old for that bus. This is much more suitable for people of our age."

Rosamund Garth looked round her with apprehension.

"It looks very comfy, but what about spiders and beetles?" she asked doubtfully.

"The beetles are only the garden kind," answered Dimsie soothingly, "and they're not nearly so bad 'cause they lead a clean outdoor life. And as for spiders – well, spiders are just as you look at them, you know. I don't believe anyone need be frightened of them if they only make up their minds not to be."

Rosamund, looking as though she found this philosophy beyond her, sat down gingerly on an upturned flowerpot, while the others crowded in, and Erica prepared to address the meeting.

"My friends," she began impressively, "we are gathered here together today to protest against – against a lot of silly twaddle, and to form ourselves into a union for our own protection – in case we get like those idiots, you see."

"But *we'd* never get like them," objected Jean.

"Well, Mabs Hunter's mother says all girls do, and if that's the case we can't to be too careful. My friends," resumed Erica, "I propose that we call our union the Anti-Soppist Society."

"Hear, hear!" responded Pamela, thumping on the hard earthen floor with the remains of an old rake.

"A jolly good idea!" agreed Dimsie.

"I have here with me," proceeded Erica, waving a sheet of paper, "the rules of our society, my friends, which, with your permission, I shall now read to you, and if there's anything you don't like you'd better say so at once, or forever after hold your peace."

The company settled down more comfortably on their respective flowerpots to listen.

"Rule One," read Erica. "No one belonging to the Anti-Soppists is on any account to give flowers to the teachers or seniors – not even any wild flowers you may find on the downs.

"Two. No member of this society must borrow things off a senior and sleep with them under her pillow. (That's what Winnie Hatton did – she borrowed a scarf off Meg Flynn last week and kept it under her pillow; a girl in her dorm told me so.)

"Three. Every member must solemnly promise not to go around kissing people . . ."

"Oh, that's not fair!" cried Pam beseechingly. "I must be allowed to kiss Roger Musgrave if I want to – just his lovely brown velvet head."

"Of course, I wasn't talking about dogs," replied Erica with dignity, "though Miss Rankin says it's a most unpleasant habit, and personally I think it's just another kind of soppiness."

"Well, Lesley Musgrave does it herself, and you couldn't call her soppy," said Pamela, defending herself.

"Roger is her own dog, which makes a difference. Anyhow, you can kiss beasts, so long as you don't kiss teachers or seniors, or things like that."

"What's the next rule, Eric?" inquired Dimsie, that point being settled.

"There aren't any more," responded Erica, folding up the paper, and taking her seat among them. "Not at present, I mean, because I really can't think of all the silly things that come into the heads of people like Joan and Winnie; but if we see them doing anything particularly loony we can make another rule about it, and meantime we've got to keep these."

"It won't be very difficiult," said Pamela with a sigh of relief. "And what's to happen if anybody did break them? Rosamund might, you know."

"I shan't!" protested Rosamund indignantly.

Erica knitted her brows over this problem.

"I shall have to think about it," she said. "Of course, you're quite right, Pam – we can't have rules without punishments – but I didn't remember that part of it. Now, does anyone else want to say anything before we break up the council?"

Mabs Hunter's hand went up.

"Yes, I do," she said demurely. "I've got a piece of news for you."

"Let's have it then," cried the others promptly.

"I don't know whether you'll like it or not," said Mabs. "I expect most of you will, but there won't be much time left for acting or playing records."

"Oh, get on, Mabs!" implored Jean. "You do ramble on so!"

"Well," said Mabs, "Sylvia Drummond has posted a notice on the hall board – I saw it on my way here – and there's to be cricket practice for the Lower School every evening from five to six, with one of the prefects in charge."

"Terrific!" cried Pam and Jean, who were both keen on cricket. "When does it begin? Not tonight? We shall have missed half of it . . ."

"No, no! Not till Wednesday. Isn't it marvellous?" declared Mabs. "I wonder what put it into Sylvia's head."

"It must have been what we said to her on Saturday, Jean," observed Erica. "You know – when you and Ros and I met her in the wood. Well, I'm jolly glad. Acting's all right in winter, but I must say I like something different in the summer term, and the tennis courts are nearly always busy. Oh – but won't Nita Tomlinson be furious!"

"Sylvia's more than a match for Nita Tomlinson," returned Jean, with the conviction of past experience.

"I wish Primrose was," declared Rosamund suddenly. "I believe she's as miserable as anything about the way Nita's taking Meg Flynn away from her. Meg has always come to us for a week in the Easter holidays, and this year she went to stay with Nita instead."

"What a shame!" said Dimsie sympathetically. "I can't think what Meg can see in Nita. I've never been able to stand her since she was so horrible to my cousin Daphne last winter. I don't really know now what it was all about, and I can't get Daph to tell me, but I'm positive Nita was at the bottom of it."

"I know, that's what we all thought," answered Erica, as they trooped out together into the sunshine. "But I'm sorry about poor Primrose. Hey, Rosamund, why does she let Nita steal her friend? Why doesn't she try to get her back?"

"I don't know," said Rosamund, shaking her yellow curls.

"I expect she takes after you a lot," was Jean's explanation. "You'd never get on if you hadn't got us to push you, and the other big girls don't seem to think of pushing Primrose. I suppose it's never occurred to them. Let's go and watch the tennis for a bit."

They went upwards through the larches, chattering together, happily unaware that Primrose herself had been on the other side of the hedge behind the tool shed, and had overheard the end of their conversation.

"There's something in what that kid said," the senior admitted to herself, flushing a little. "Why don't I try to win Meg back? I've a jolly good mind to try if I can think of a way to do it without exactly swallowing my pride. If only I was good at games it might give me a pull over Nita, but I'm useless at anything except cricket. I wonder . . ."

A sudden light dawned on her troubled face, and she wandered towards the nets, her hands clasped behind her back, her shady hat tilted over her eyes.

"That might do it," she said at last aloud. "Anyhow, I can try."

# CHAPTER 5

# CONCERNING CRICKET

Preparation at the Jane Willard filled a good deal of time during the winter, but when the summer term came round it was reduced to a minimum. Even the Sixth Form could finish their work by tea time, and be free to spend the cooler hours of the day out of doors.

On the afternoon which saw the founding of the Anti-Soppist Society in the tool shed, Meg Flynn was alone in the senior schoolroom after tea, finishing some algebra which had taken rather longer than usual to solve, when the door opened and banged abruptly again after Nita Tomlinson.

The games-captain was a small, dark girl with a sallow, ill-tempered face which was not improved, at the present moment, by the thunderous scowl she wore. Meg looked across at her in some trepidation, and then observed mildly:

"I'm nearly ready, Nita. Won't you go on and ask two of the others to make up a set with us?"

But Nita threw herself down on the battered old couch which stood in a corner beyond the line of desks, and her racket clattered to the floor at her feet.

"No," she said. "I don't feel like tennis this afternoon."

"But, sure, and we fixed it up only half an hour ago," Meg pointed out in amazement, "and you've brought your racket down."

"I know," said Nita sulkily, "I meant to play, but the truth is, Meg, I saw that notice of Sylvia Drummond's on the board in the hall, and it has annoyed me so much that I can't think of anything else."

"Oh, I know!" responded Meg. "I saw it, too. But after

all, Nita, what's the harm? The poor kids ought to have a game sometimes, and if there's a senior in charge they can't do much damage to the pitch."

But Nita apparently did not see it in that light.

"The point is," she said emphatically, sitting up and crossing her feet in front of her, "am I to be games-captain, or am I not? I said that the Lower School were not to use our pitch nor to play cricket at all unless they were properly coached. I'm only thinking of the future teams who will have to play for the school. If those kids mess about by themselves they will pick up all sorts of tiresome tricks both in batting and bowling which will all need to be unlearnt later on."

If Meg thought privately that the cricket of the future was not Nita's business she knew better than to say so; instead she tried another tack.

"But at that rate, Nita, the poor little things would never be getting a game at all, and that means losing a lot of pleasure. Miss Yelland has no time to spare for them when she has got to get us in trim for the fixtures, and it seems you don't consider any of the Sixth Form instructing them."

"Certainly not," retorted Nita, "unless it's you or me, and neither of us can waste time fussing over a bunch of infants. We've got to win the doubles championship at tennis, and then we'll need plenty of practice, since that will mean playing for Jane's. As for Sylvia Drummond, I'll let her know what I think of her interference!"

"Will you?" asked a calm, lazy voice from the open window, and Sylvia strolled in, fanning herself with her broad-brimmed hat. "Phew! It's hot on the courts today! Well, Nita, let's have it, then. What do you think of my interference?"

Nita flushed hotly under sallow skin. She detested the headgirl with her cool sarcasm and the nonchalant drawl in which she generally voiced it. Above all things, Nita hated being laughed at, for she had grand ideas concerning her own importance, and resented her failure to impress Sylvia. She threw up her head now, looking not unlike an impudent little house sparrow, and retorted:

"As I am captain of games, I must say I can't see what right you have to make arrangements for the juniors' cricket.

You might, at least, have consulted me before pinning up that notice in the hall."

"But I understood," said Sylvia in assumed surprise, "that you had no time to attend to such mundane matters. There are the tennis tournaments coming off in a fortnight, and the first eleven to work up before the cricket matches are played. If you feel such a responsibility towards the kids, aren't you glad to share it?"

"That's just what I complain of!" cried Nita angrily. "You haven't allowed me a share or a say in the matter! You tell me this – what benevolent seniors are going to look after those kids from five to six every evening, when, as you say, the school tournaments are coming off so soon?"

"Oh, that's all right – we're not all competing! Daphne, Joyce and I are each keeping an eye on them for one evening, and Primrose Garth is taking them on for the remaining three."

"Primrose Garth!" sneered Nita. "I should think she isn't competing! Have you ever seen her serve?"

Sylvia remained silent, but she turned her gaze towards Meg with a placid smile, as much as to say, "Primrose is your friend – it's not my business to defend her."

Meg understood, and coloured uncomfortably.

"She's jolly good at cricket, anyhow," she said abruptly. "The kids won't pick up any bad style from her, Nita."

Nita shrugged her shoulders.

"That's a matter of opinion," she declared.

"Excuse me," interposed Sylvia, "but it's nothing of the sort – it's a matter of fact. You've only got to ask Miss Yelland what she thinks of Primrose's batting. She's got by far the hardest drive of any girl at Jane's."

Nita sprang to her feet, and picked up her racket.

"Oh, all right," she replied sulkily. "Have it your own way. I suppose the next thing will be a Lower School eleven with a fixture card of its own – making a fool of Jane's all over the county!"

"It's not a bad idea, Nita," said Sylvia meditatively. "Thanks very much. Not for the last clause, of course, but that wouldn't be a necessary result."

Nita strode towards the window with blazing eyes.

"Come along, Meg!" she flung back over her shoulder. "There's a vacant court now, and if we don't hurry up it will be bagged. We've wasted quite enough time, as it is, chattering in here!"

Sylvia followed them slowly out onto the terrace, then made her way towards a group of chairs under the trees.

"I fear Nita Tomlinson is annoyed with me," she remarked mildly to a tall, dark girl with glasses, who was reading in a hammock.

"I suppose you mean about this cricket business?" asked Joyce, laying down her book with a yawn. "You don't look very sorry, somehow."

"I can't say that I am," Sylvia grinned. "My sympathies are entirely with the kids, but for goodness sake, don't let them muck up that precious pitch when you're in charge, or I believe Nita will lie in wait and murder me, some dark night, in the wood."

Joyce laughed.

"You'd better look out," she returned, half in earnest. "We all know how careful Nita is to pay people back when she thinks they've put one cross her, and she must have stacked up quite a few grudges against you by now. Remember how Daphne suffered at her hands last Christmas term."

"I'm not likely to forget that in a hurry!" said Sylvia in a sudden blaze of wrath which contrasted curiously with her usual unruffled demeanour. "But she won't try that little game with me," she added, relapsing into her ordinary tones. "She saw once before that it didn't pay. Really, you know, Joyce, that girl has an extraordinarily spiteful nature. I've never met anything quite like it."

"And I'm sure I never want to!" Joyce rejoined. "Have you got her totted down in that note-book of yours, where you collect character-sketches for your future literary career?"

Sylvia chuckled.

"You bet I have! Do you think I could neglect such an opportunity? She'll make a most valuable villain one of these days, when I write my famous novel. Yes, Mabs? What do you want?"

"Please, Sylvia," said Mabs Hunter, who had been

25

hanging about, waiting to deliver her message, "the others sent me to ask you if we may bat at the nets, so as to get some practice before Wednesday?"

"Of course you can," said Sylvia. "As long as none of the eleven require them at present. Empty out of that hammock, Joyce, you lazy cow. You've had it ever since tea, and it's my turn now."

# CHAPTER 6

# THE GREEN
# NOTE-BOOK

The juniors took to cricket with an enthusiasm which was greatly stimulated by Nita Tomlinson's evident disgust. Jean was discovered to be a steady bat for her age, and Pamela was an agile fielder with the makings of a bowler, while one or two girls in the Lower Fourth were shaping up well. The young Third Formers were eager to learn, but so far they had failed to distinguish themselves greatly.

Of the seniors who coached them, Primrose was by far the most painstaking. In addition to their hour on the pitch before it was claimed by the other girls, she was always ready to give instruction at the nets to anybody who wanted it, and it was really owing to Primrose that Jean and Pamela made so much progress.

"I've got a scheme, kids," she announced one evening, as they walked up from the field together after a strenuous session. "I mean to work you like slaves till half-term, and then I shall pick a team from among you, appoint a captain, and leave her to challenge the Middle School."

An audible gasp ran through the ranks about her.

"Jean Gordon will be captain," piped a shrill voice in the rear. "I'm sure she will."

"Very likely," responded Primrose, "if she goes on as she's doing, but I can't decide that or anything else yet. I shan't pick anybody at all till half-term, and that will give everybody a chance to show what they can do."

"But the Middle School!" murmured Joan Hardy in tones of awe. "I mean – we'd never beat them!"

"Who can tell?" said Primrose encouragingly. "At least

you can give a good account of yourselves. Remember that, at present, half the school don't know you can play at all. You've got to show them you can, and do me credit. I'm very anxious you should do me credit, kids.''

"And so we jolly well will!" cried Pamela impulsively, while Betty Grey pressed closer and hung on to the big girl's arm, at which Erica Innes scowled forbiddingly. "It's awfully nice of you to take so much trouble over us, Primrose. We'll show the Middle School what you've taught us – see if we don't!"

Primrose reddened.

"It isn't particularly nice of me – it's as much for my own sake as for yours," she answered hurriedly, and shaking them off she went in search of Joyce Lamond, who had promised to take a ramble with her on the downs before supper.

Erica Innes and her faithful five sat on the grass at the side of the courts to watch the tennis. Play-acting was out of fashion with them at present, and sports were the new craze, so the possibilities of the tennis championship came in for their careful consideration.

"Your cousin will win the singles again, Dimsie," Erica prophesied. "No one in Jane's can stand up to Daphne there, but I'm afraid Meg and Nita will get the doubles. Nita's made up her mind about that and she keeps Meg hard at it."

"Who's Daphne playing with in the doubles? Sylvia? Oh, Sylvia's terrific. Why shouldn't they win it?"

"Well, they don't seem to have much time to play together – at least, Sylvia doesn't. I suppose it's being headgirl, but she has so many different things to attend to."

"I know something about Sylvia," remarked Mabs Hunter in her most mysterious manner.

"What? What? Do tell us!"

"Hurry up now, Mabs! Is it really interesting?"

"Yes – awfully. You know she's going to be an author when she grows up?"

The others assented. Sylvia's literary ambitions had leaked out some time ago, and Jane's had felt certain of their fulfilment since last term, when their headgirl had won a prize in an open essay competition, for which schools had entered from all over the country. It had been something of an astonishment to her teachers, for Sylvia had not hitherto distinguished herself in this line, but Miss Yorke had put it down to the fact that the given subject had admitted of a character study, and apparently Sylvia had a flair for that sort of thing.

"I've discovered how she trains for it," Mabs told them importantly. "She's got a note-book, and she describes us all in it – everybody in Jane's, even Nita Tomlinson – not only our outsides, but our insides, too . . ."

"Huh!" interposed Erica scornfully. "I knew you'd got hold of the wrong end of the stick! That's her human biology notes. All the Sixth Form have them, with lovely little drawings in coloured felt-tips of people's digestions and things like that. I saw Meg's once, when she left it lying about."

"I don't mean that at all!" cried Mabs indignantly. "It's people's characters, not their digestions – just what Sylvia thinks we're really like. It must be terrifically interesting. I really would like to see it."

"So would I," echoed Rosamund. "Do you think she'd show it to us, if we asked her?"

"No way," said Jean brusquely. "Besides, I bet it'd be very dull, wouldn't it, Dimsie?"

"Horribly," assented Dimsie. "Let's go and do something now. I'm tired of sitting about."

"I'll come in a minute," said Rosamund, "but Primrose is just going to play Cecil Hepworth, and I want to watch her."

The others disappeared in a body through the fir trees, and Rosamund, turning her head for a moment to watch them go, saw Nita Tomlinson lolling back in a deck-chair close behind her, her racket lying on the grass by her side.

"Well, now," she said, regarding Rosamund good-naturedly through half-closed eyes, "so you'd like to see that green note-book of Sylvia's, would you? She's rather shy about it, though. I don't suppose she'd let anyone but Daphne Maitland see it. Still – you could, if you liked, you know."

"How could I?" asked Rosamund, gazing up at her with innocent blue eyes.

"Well, Sylvia keeps it lying on her study table. Anyone can read it, if they take the trouble to fetch it."

"But," said Rosamund, looking puzzled, "if Sylvia doesn't want to show it to anyone, that wouldn't be right, would it? It would be like – like reading somebody else's letters."

"Oh, I don't think so," said Nita carelessly. "She may be too shy to show it, but she wouldn't mind people looking at it. Heavens! If she's going to write books I suppose she'll want people to read them!"

"Yes, but that's different," replied Rosamund, though she did not attempt to explain why.

"Oh, well – do as you like," said Nita, shrugging her shoulders. "I expect Sylvia would feel greatly flattered, as a matter of fact, if she knew the interest which some of you take in that green note-book of hers." She regarded the younger girl on the grass slyly through her lashes. "How goes the cricket?" she inquired next, somewhat abruptly.

Rosamund looked astonished, for she imagined this to be delicate ground with the games-captain; the Lower School were well aware that they used the pitch in spite of Nita, rather than with her approval, and this seemed a strange subject to introduce. However, she answered that and other questions on the matter, and presently found herself chattering away as gaily as though this unpopular senior had been Daphne Maitland or Meg Flynn. Rosamund was a friendly little soul whose confidence was easily won, and she felt rather proud that Nita should pay so much attention to her. The elder girl could be very charming when she liked, and she was deliberately setting out now to captivate Rosamund. They were on very friendly terms, half an hour later, when Dimsie, pushing through the rhododendron bushes behind them, came in search of her friend.

"Rosamund!" she said peremptorily. "Come on – we were waiting for you. Erica has thought of a terrific new game."

Rosamund jumped up at once and ran after her. She had had enough of Nita for the time being; nevertheless, she took up the cudgels in her defence when Dimsie said angrily:

"What made you stay behind and talk to that Nita Tomlinson, when you know how we all can't stand her? What was she saying to you?"

"Lots of things. She's really quite nice when you get to know her, Dimsie. She asked me all about the cricket, and I don't think she minds us playing a bit. I rather like her, actually," she added with a touch of defiance.

"Oh, do you?" retorted Dimsie. "Well, you can't, then, 'cause none of the rest of us do! I simply don't know what Erica would say if she heard you."

Rosamund sighed plaintively. Their leader's authority was never questioned by her five faithful followers.

"There was only one thing about Nita that seemed to me a little bit funny," she confessed. "She said if I wanted to see that note-book of Sylvia's, all I'd got to do was to go to her study table and take it. She made it sound all right, but somehow I don't think it would have been."

Dimsie stood still abruptly and gasped.

"I should think not! I'm glad you had the sense not to listen to her. Honestly, Ros, surely that shows you what she's really like?"

"Oh, I don't know," returned Rosamund with all the obstinacy of a gentle nature. "I don't think she's half as bad as you all make her out."

# CHAPTER 7

# "NITA'S LATEST"

"Hey, Sylvia!" Primrose put her head round the door of the study which Sylvia and Daphne shared. "Are you doing anything this evening? Will you come out on the cliffs with me?"

Sylvia looked up from the book over which she was poring, and tossed her fair hair back from her face.

"I'd love to," she said, "if you can wait till I get this history fixed in my brain. I really don't know how Miss Yorke expected us to do all this by tomorrow."

"I thought she'd overshot the mark a bit," assented Primrose, "but I suppose she was tempted to polish off Anne's reign. Bring it out with you and finish it on the downs."

"No way," said Sylvia decidedly. "The affairs of Anne's day wouldn't go with the sea breezes and the wild thyme. You want Elizabeth I for that, or the Stuarts. Sit down and amuse yourself with Daphne's library book – I shan't be long."

"What queer ideas you have!" observed Primrose when at last the history book was closed with a bang, and Sylvia pushed back her chair. "Though I think I know what you mean about Elizabeth I and the sea breezes. Have you written any verses this term?"

"Not many," said Sylvia. "It's easier to do prose at school – verse in the holidays."

"Let's see what you have done, anyhow," begged Primrose. "You can read it to me under the old lighthouse."

Sylvia laughed, and caught up two green-covered notebooks which lay on the table.

"You won't think much of them," she declared. "At least, if you do, it will reveal your bad taste. This isn't one of your evenings on duty with the juniors?"

"No," said Primrose, "Joyce is taking them. They're coming on rather well, you know, and they're all madly enthusiastic, except – well, except my small sister."

Sylvia gave her a quick look of surprise.

"Rosamund? But she was doing rather well, I thought. Last time I had them, she took a catch – and held it too. What's the matter with Rosamund?"

"That's what I want to talk to you about," returned Primrose, and led the way by a path which skirted the wood and playing field, taking them out into the grassy valley beyond. Opposite, abruptly, rose the down, whose further side dropped over in high chalk cliffs washed by the Channel waves.

The girls talked very little as they breasted the steep slope towards the disused lighthouse, crushing the small-leaved thyme underfoot on their way. Sylvia could see that her companion was perturbed, and wondered inwardly what fresh trouble had arisen.

"I should like to shake that idiot Meg Flynn!" was her mental comment on the situation, but she soon learnt that Meg was not the cause of worry this time.

Primrose dropped on the wind-bitten turf where the wall surrounding the old lighthouse cast a strip of shade.

"I didn't realize it had been so hot lately," she remarked. "Look at this great crack in the ground!"

"That's not the heat," replied Sylvia, throwing herself down beside her. "I've noticed that crack before. It's a natural fissure of some sort, and it's quite deep. Once I slipped my hand into it, and I couldn't feel the bottom."

"I expect it goes down into the cliff," said Primrose idly. "Somebody told me once that there was a smugglers' cave round here somewhere. Listen, Sylvia! I wanted to have a good talk with you where there was no danger of being interrupted by any of the others."

"So I gathered," returned Sylvia, lying back on the grass with her hat pulled over her face.

"Have you heard Nita's latest?"

Sylvia shrugged her shoulders as well as her position would allow.

"I really don't know. Nita is far too deep for a simple-minded creature like myself! Is it anything worse than usual?"

"Well, I think it is," Primrose answered in troubled tones. "She's trying to get a hold over Rosamund."

"What?" Sylvia shot up into a sitting position and glared indignantly. "Is she trying the Jean Gordon game over again? The result of that affair ought to have taught her a lesson, if anything would."

"I don't know," said Primrose despondently, "but for some reason best known to herself she's trying to win Rosamund's favour, and she seems to be succeeding too. The child's rather conceited, and I think Nita butters her up a bit. Anyhow, she can twist her round her little finger now."

"How did you find it out?" asked Sylvia, looking grave. She had reason to distrust Nita's influence over any of the younger girls.

"She skipped cricket on two of my evenings, and Mabs Hunter told me she was with Nita somewhere. So I asked her about it – Rosamund, I mean -- and she said she was helping Nita to develop her photos in the dark room, and that it was better fun than cricket."

"And what else?" inquired Sylvia, watching a blue-black cloud which was creeping slowly up out of the sea.

"Oh, I've noticed Rosamund hanging round her in the garden and fielding her balls at tennis. Nita may be a pain to us, Sylvia, but it's astonishing how she manages to charm any girl she chooses, big or small. First it was Meg, and now Rosamund."

"But I can't understand it," protested Sylvia in bewilderment. "What's she trying to do? There's nothing she can hope to gain from Rosamund's favour. She has no known grudge against you, and if she has, surely she must feel she's paying you back through Meg."

"She certainly is!" exclaimed Primrose, with a touch of bitterness. "You know, Sylvia, Meg and I have always walked to church together ever since we came to Jane's, and now – for the last two Sundays – she's told me she was going with Nita!"

Sylvia nodded. She had noticed the new arrangement, and had guessed how Primrose felt, but she could think of no consolation to offer. In her heart of hearts she asked the same question as Erica Innes: "Why did Primrose not make some attempt to win Meg back from Nita?"

"You'd better talk to Rosamund," she said at last. "Being her sister, you've got some right to interfere. Can't you tell her that you don't think your parents would want her hanging round a girl like Nita Tomlinson? She's a nice little kid, Rosamund. I shouldn't think she'd be difficult to manage."

"You don't know her," said Primrose, smiling. "She's very sweet, but as obstinate as a mule. However, I can try."

"And if I catch her cutting the cricket practice when I take it tomorrow, I'll pull her up sharp. Hey, Primrose, I believe we'd better make tracks. There's going to be an awful storm in a minute. I've been watching it coming up over the sea while we talked."

Primrose looked up, and sprang to her feet, as a threatening rumble of thunder rolled across the sky.

"Oh, come on!" she said nervously. "I hate being out in it, and these cliffs do echo so!"

Sylvia followed her more reluctantly, with a backward glance at the panorama of cloud lit for a second by a darting bayonet of lightning. Far out in the Channel a solitary white sail made the inky shades of sea and sky look blacker by comparison.

"I'd like to stay and watch it," she said wistfully, "but we'd be drenched to the skin if we did. All right, Primrose, I'm coming. Come on – I'll race you down into the valley."

Primrose was ready to agree to anything at that moment which meant an increase of speed. Spurred on by another angry growl from the darkness behind them, they started to run with a series of flying leaps and bounds, gaining rapid impetus owing to the steepness of the descent. Unluckily, the short thyme-spread turf was slippery from the long drought, and Sylvia, losing her footing suddenly, half fell, half rolled down the remainder of the slope, pulling Primrose with her. They lay still for a moment, too breathless to speak; then Sylvia sat up, looking a little white and shaken.

"Jack and Jill fell down the hill," she observed whimsically, "but I'm afraid, in this case, it isn't Jack's crown which has suffered. If you're all right, Primrose, can you help me? I

35

seem to have given my foot a bit of a twist."

Primrose picked herself up quite uninjured, and turned to give a helping hand to her companion.

"Hurry up, Sylvia!" she urged. "That was a horrid flash just now."

Sylvia made a painful effort to struggle to her feet.

"I – I'm trying," she responded bravely. "Hold on a minute – I . . ."

And then, quite quietly, to Primrose's horror she fainted away, just as a great crash seemed to shake the little valley from end to end.

# CHAPTER 8

# A MEETING IN COUNCIL

"Are we all here?" Erica Innes surveyed the meeting assembled in the tool shed, and took note of its members. "Dimsie, Pamela, Jean, Mabs – yes, that's right. Right, then."

She seated herself on the largest and most comfortable flowerpot, reserved by right of seniority for the president of the society, and prepared to open the proceedings.

"Hold on, Erica! Rosamund isn't here yet," objected Dimsie. "I looked for her on my way down, but she didn't seem to be anywhere about."

"No," replied Erica significantly. "I half thought she wouldn't be, though I sent the fiery cross round during maths, and she was there all right."

"Are you sure that wasn't just when she went to her music lesson?" asked Dimsie eagerly. "You know she had to go ten minutes earlier today."

"She was there when the cross went round," replied Jean briefly. "I passed it to her."

"And I know where she is now," added Mabs Hunter meaningfully.

"So do I," retorted Erica. "At least I've got a pretty good idea. Keeping guard over Nita Tomlinson's negatives to see they don't get over-printed, right?"

Mabs nodded.

"Right," she assented. "On the terrace, by the verandah steps."

There was a moment's pause, during which Dimsie fidgeted with her sandal and tried to think of excuses for the absent Rosamund. She guessed that her friend's case was to be brought up for judgement, and feared that she herself was likely to be sole counsel for the defence.

"Well," began Erica, at last, shaking herself out a little, and settling more firmly on the flowerpot, "since all of us are here who mean to come, we may as well get to business. My friends," adopting her official voice, "we are met here together this afternoon to hold an inquiry into a very sad case which I expect you know all about. I refer, friends and sisters, to one of our number who is absent from our midst. You have just heard where she is, and what she is doing. Have any of you got anything to say about it?"

"Rosamund's awfully absent-minded," broke in Dimsie hurriedly. "I expect she's forgotten all about it – or – or perhaps she didn't make out the time of the meeting properly. You didn't write it very distinctly, you know, Erica."

Erica waved these excuses aside with a stately gesture.

"The rest of you made it out right enough," she returned. "Rosamund's no more stupid than you or Pam. To resume, my friends – am I not correct in stating that we've all got a sort of feeling inside us regarding this absent member?"

"I haven't!" protested Dimsie indignantly.

"All right – Dimsie Maitland hasn't. What about you, Pamela? Jean? Mabs?"

"I always had my doubts about Rosamund," replied Pam gloomily. "I had an idea she might go and turn soppy if she wasn't careful."

"She knows she has," added downright Jean, "otherwise she wouldn't have tried to dodge this meeting."

"She hasn't done anything of the kind!" burst forth Dimsie again.

"Then why isn't she here, if you know such a lot about it?" demanded Erica.

"I've told you why," Dimsie answered, glancing wildly round the council chamber for inspiration, and finding it in a thick cobweb which festooned one corner. "Or perhaps it's because of the spiders and things. You know what a little funk she is about spiders."

"She's managed to put up with these till today," rejoined Erica drily, "and none of them are very big when you come to

look them in the face. No, Dimsie! You know the truth as well as
any of us. Our absent member, dear friends, is not present
because she is no longer a member, and she can't hide it from
her own conscience."

"That's just it," agreed Jean briefly.

Mabs nodded.

"Rosamund isn't an anti now – she's a feeble soppist, as
bad as Winnie Hatton, and worse than Betty Grey."

"Worse than anybody in the whole school," amended
Pamela. "Whoever heard of anyone doing favours for Nita
Tomlinson?"

"But it isn't fair!" cried Dimsie desperately. "Ros hasn't
broken any of the rules. You know she hasn't."

"Yes, she has," returned Erica promptly.

"She hasn't kissed anyone, nor given them flowers, nor
slept with their belongings under her pillow."

"No, but she has fielded a senior's tennis balls, and run
errands for her, hasn't she? Of course she has! We've all seen
her."

"But those things aren't . . ." began Dimsie.

"Yes, they are," Erica cut in. "I made a new rule about
them last night. You can't say we didn't all agree that the rules
would have to be added to when fresh sillinesses happened that
we hadn't thought of forbidding. And it's nonsense to say
Rosamund didn't know," she added hastily, as Dimsie's mouth
opened again. "Of course she knew, or she wouldn't look so
guilty and keep out of our way. She felt she was breaking the
spirit of the rules, and you know what Miss Yorke told us in her
speech on the first day, that it was far worse to break the spirit of
the rules than just the rules themselves."

Dimsie felt there was some flaw in this line of argument,
but she was no match for the fluent Erica, and things were
evidently looking black for the criminal whom she was seeking
to defend.

"But what are you going to do about it?" she asked
anxiously.

"I don't know," admitted the president of the Anti-
Soppists. "Of course she can't be in our society any more, but
that isn't enough. I shall have to think of a punishment now that

you all see she's guilty, and then I'll have another council and let you know."

"We might send her to Coventry," suggested Mabs helpfully, but Erica shook her head.

"Certainly not," she said decidedly. "That's been done too often before. If I think up a punishment I make it nice and original. Hey! Was that thunder?"

The Anti-Soppists scurried out of their lair in time to see a jagged fork of lightning split the black cloud which had gathered over the sea, and was now towering in purple bastions above the green shoulder of the down. The rest of the society apparently shared Primrose Garth's views concerning thunder, for the next heavy rumbling sent them flying up the path to seek shelter indoors; but Dimsie, regardless of possible danger, crept to the edge of the trees and waited to see the next flash. From where she stood the whole bare hillside was stretched out before her, and presently she caught sight of the two seniors hurrying over the crest.

"I wonder who that is," she thought, as she watched their leaping, bounding descent. "The tall one looks like Sylvia – I'm sure it's her green cotton dress; she always wears green – but the other – oh, what a laugh! They're rolling over and over down the hill!"

Dimsie's merriment changed to dismay, however, when she saw Sylvia's vain attempt to rise, and her limp collapse at Primrose's feet.

"She's hurt herself," thought Dimsie. "Oh lor'! I'd better see if I can help."

Heedless of the thunder, which seemed now to be crashing right overhead, Dimsie darted across the empty playing field, from which the cricketers had long since fled, and over the rough tussocks of grass beyond the fence which separated the grounds of Jane's from the downs.

"It's all right," she panted cheerfully, as she arrived within earshot. "I'm coming. I'll help you. Has she fainted, or what?"

"Oh dear! What'll I do?" cried Primrose, who was fluttering distractedly over Sylvia's prostrate form. "It's her foot – I'm afraid she's hurt herself very badly. Oh, what'll I do? That lightning's awful!"

The small girl took command of the situation promptly, for she judged from the state of Primrose's nerves that there was no point looking to her for help.

"The best thing you can do," she replied briskly, "is to run up to the house as fast as you can and ask matron to come, and old Vicars. They'd better bring something to carry Sylvia on if her foot's bad; she's probably sprained it. We *could* carry her back queen's-chair way – you know, linking arms under her – but we're not quite the same height," regarding the tall senior thoughtfully, "and I'm afraid it might bump her rather. Hurry up, will you, Primrose? The rain may come on any minute now."

No need to tell Primrose to hurry. She did pause for a moment to argue the point with this exceedingly determined junior, whom it hardly seemed right to leave in a thunderstorm with an unconscious charge, but Dimsie soon disposed of her objections.

"You couldn't do a bit of good here," she said with more truth than politeness. "You're frightened, and I'm not. Only do be quick about it, and send someone before we're both soaked through."

An extra vivid flash proved an even more convincing argument than any of Dimsie's. Primrose delayed no longer, but ran off at top-speed across the grass tussocks.

# CHAPTER 9

# ROSAMUND'S ERRAND

No sooner had Primrose left them than Dimsie set about doing what she could in the way of first aid. It was easy enough to discover which foot was injured, for the instep had begun to swell above the ankle strap. Dimsie decided to remove the sandal in order to relieve the pressure on the swelling ankle. Very carefully, very gently, she managed to unbuckle the tight ankle-strap, and prepared to ease the sandal off Sylvia's limp foot. At this juncture, to her great relief, Sylvia stirred and opened her eyes. For a moment she lay staring at her attendant in silent surprise, then she asked feebly:

"What on earth are you doing here, Dimsie? Where's Primrose?"

"Gone up to the school for help," explained Dimsie briefly, much occupied with the sandal. "You see, you couldn't walk across the rough ground with a foot like this. I'm not hurting you, am I, Sylvia?"

"Not really," answered Sylvia with a wry smile, "but I feel as though you were. Never mind, Dimsie – get on with the good work. I'm quite aware that the shoe must come off, and it would hurt, at present, if anybody so much as looked at that ankle."

"Is it so awfully bad?" asked Dimsie sympathetically. "I'm very sorry, Sylvia. I know it ought to be bathed with the coldest water, but there's none nearer than the house unless the rain comes on."

"And that," said her patient, "is not to be desired at present. Aren't you afraid of all that thunder, Dimsie?"

"Not a bit," she said. "I like it. But I wish they'd be quick, because I *don't* like it when it rains. It would be horrible for you to have to lie there in a puddle."

"I shan't do anything of the sort," Sylvia assured her with returning vigour. "First of all I'm going to sit up, and then perhaps you could help me to stand."

"Not with that foot!" cried Dimsie in horror. "Oh, here they come! I can see Matron's white dress among the trees."

The first heavy drops fell as the rescuers arrived, and the whole party were uncomfortably damp before they reached shelter, but Dimsie ran off to change her wet clothes in a glow of satisfaction, for Matron had praised her warmly for having had the sense to remove Sylvia's shoe.

"I can't understand what Primrose Garth was thinking of not to do it as soon as she fainted, but apparently her presence of mind isn't proof against a thunderstorm," Matron remarked. "It's a blessing that child came upon the scene before the ankle had swollen much further. As it is, you will have to take it easy for a week or two, Sylvia. This is a nasty sprain."

"Oh, hard luck, Sylvia!" commiserated Daphne Maitland, who had come up to the sanatorium to make inquiries. "You're always getting knocked out, one way or another; last autumn you had that bad knee which spoilt the hockey season for you, and now this! Here ends our partnership for the mixed doubles!"

"You hadn't much chance, anyhow," returned Sylvia with resignation, "when you insisted on having me for your partner. Meg and Nita, at least, were bound to beat us. No – what I'm really bothered about is the cricket match against Westover High School, for – though I say it myself – I *am* one of our best bats."

"You certainly are," agreed Daphne readily, "and Cecil Hepworth heard from her cousin at Westover that they've got a particularly strong batting side there this term."

"Oh dear!" groaned Sylvia.

"When is this match coming off?" inquired Matron, busying herself with cold compresses on a small table which had been wheeled up beside the couch.

"The twenty-eighth – in about ten days," replied Daphne.

"Well, of course you couldn't play by then," decreed Matron judically, as she wrung out the dripping bandage. "At least, I mean, you couldn't dash about; but I see no reason why you shouldn't be able to bat if someone else will run for you."

"Great!" cried Daphne. "One of the kids could do it, Sylvia. What they lack in judgement they make up for in speed."

"I don't know if it's allowable," Sylvia said doubtfully, "and, anyhow, Nita may prefer to put someone else in, but I'll talk to her about it. If you're going down to the Sixth Form room now, Daph, you might ask her to pop up and see me before supper."

As Joyce Lamond had observed, there were many long-cherished grudges which Nita was anxious to pay off against the headgirl, but, to do her justice, she never allowed her private grievances to interfere with Jane's prowess at games; so she was genuinely distressed to hear of Sylvia's accident, and obeyed her summons to the sanatorium with all speed.

"I think it could be managed," she said, when she had heard Sylvia's suggestion. "Of course, it isn't strictly correct, but we let Westover do something very similar last year, so I don't see how they can object. Anyhow, I'll write straight off to their captain this evening and ask her."

"Do," said Sylvia in relieved tones. "It was Matron's idea and I can't think of a better one. I don't think Tony Semple would make much of a substitute; tennis is her game. Hey, there's the sun coming out! That storm isn't going to break the weather after all, though it looked like it as it came across the Channel. Oh, blast!"

"What's the matter?" asked Nita, who was preparing to take her leave. "Foot bad?"

"No, it's not that – I've just an awful thought. I took two note-books out onto the cliffs with me this afternoon, and I certainly haven't brought them back. They must have been lying at the foot of the downs in all that rain! Matron, would you mind awfully sending someone for them? I fell just at the end of the track which runs down from the old lighthouse – there's a broken post or something lying there in the grass, and the books should be somewhere near it."

"I'll go," cried Nita quickly. "No, it's no bother. I'll just have time to slip on my wellies and run across before supper.

Did you say they'd got green covers?"

"I didn't, as a matter of fact," said Sylvia, "but they have. Thanks very much, Nita, but I don't like to trouble you. Send one of the juniors."

"They never find anything they're sent for," declared Nita, making for the door. "I hope your ankle will soon be better."

Sylvia's "collection", as she called her book of character studies, had long been an object of interest and curiosity to her fellow seniors, and none of them had been more eager to see it than Nita Tomlinson. She was a vain girl, who attached an overweening importance to anything concerning herself, and she longed to see what Sylvia had written about her, even though it might not be particularly flattering. Nita was, in fact, one of those people who would rather be insulted than ignored; but she knew very well that it would be useless to plead with Sylvia for permission to look at her green note-book; they were not on terms of that sort – far from it.

Now, however, it seemed as though fortune had played into Nita's hands. Probably not another girl in Jane's would have regarded her errand in such a light, or even dreamt of opening the books which she had promised to fetch, but Nita's standard of honour was lower than that of her companions, and she only felt that this was an opportunity for her grasping. Her chagrin, therefore, may be better imagined than described when little Rosamund Garth pursued her, as she was crossing the verandah, with a message from Miss Yelland, the games-mistress.

"She wants to see you at once in the teachers' room," said Rosamund, breathless with her haste. "It's about the match with Westover, I think."

Nita stood still and stamped her foot.

"Oh, *bother!*" she exclaimed. "The gong will ring in ten minutes, and when I can get away after supper it will be too dark to find it!"

"Find what?" asked Rosamund, adding readily, "I'll go and get it, whatever it is."

The senior stared at her doubtfully for a moment.

"All right," she said slowly. "I suppose it's the only thing

45

to be done. Sylvia wants her green note-books, Rosamund – you know – the one I told you about, with the school characters in it, and another. She thinks she dropped them on the downs when she fell, beside the old post on the lighthouse path. Run and fetch them as fast as you can, but don't take them to Sylvia – bring them straight to me directly I leave Miss Yelland."

"But – but, Nita," protested Rosamund faintly, "I don't think Sylvia – I mean, Sylvia mightn't like it."

Nita turned upon her so fiercely that the junior shrank back in haste.

"I didn't ask you what Sylvia liked or disliked – I told you what you were to do, so don't argue about it. Just do as you're told. And remember! Bring those green note-books straight to me."

Not daring to keep Miss Yelland waiting any longer, she ran back into the house, while Rosamund turned reluctant feet towards the path through the dripping larches, half hoping that someone in authority might see the direction in which she was going and call her back.

"I know it's wrong," she thought, with a growing distaste for Nita's commands. "I don't care! I'll just find the books, and take them straight to Sylvia, whatever she says!"

# CHAPTER 10

# ROSAMUND IN DISGRACE

Primrose had been right when she declared that Nita Tomlinson had been able to twist her sister round her little finger; but the spell had not been of long duration, and already Rosamund's admiration was beginning to wear thin. Nita made demands on her time and attention which were growing more and more annoying, and besides, she realized only too well that Erica Innes & Co. looked upon the alliance with disfavour. When all was said and done, Rosamund valued the opinions of the Anti-Soppists above those of anybody else, however great and powerful; moreover, she felt that there was something fishy about that last command of Nita's. The book was Sylvia Drummond's, and, according to Nita herself, it was supposed to be strictly private.

"So it isn't likely," Rosamund argued to herself, as she trotted down through the wet wood, "that she'd want Nita to have it, when everybody knows they aren't friends. I don't know why I liked Nita at first, but I've had about enough of her now – Miss Yelland said my jography was disgraceful this morning."

The connection between Nita Tomlinson and "jography" was clear enough to Rosamund herself. She had been unable, the day before, to go over her lessons with Dimsie as usual, after tea, because Nita had demanded her services as ballboy at the tennis courts, and had even refused to release her in time for the juniors' cricket practice. It was by no means the first time this had happened, and Rosamund, whose work had been improving steadily with Dimsie's help, found that she was once more slipping down-hill in the class. Altogether, Nita's favours were proving too expensive to be worth while.

The first missing note-book, with its stiff green boards, was not hard to find; it had fallen on the lee side of the old post, and only the cover had been damaged. But of the second there was no sign. Rosamund examined the ground sufficiently to satisfy herself in that respect, and then ran back across the playing field. Emerging from the wood path on to the gravelled terrace, she almost collided with Mabs Hunter, who stared at her suspiciously.

"Was that you over on the downs just now? And without your wellies, too! Well, you'll catch it from Miss Yelland in a minute! She spotted you from the verandah, and she's absolutely fuming! What made you go? You know we're not allowed out of bounds without a senior."

"It isn't any business of yours, anyhow!" snapped Rosamund crossly, pushing past her.

"But wait a minute! What are you doing with Sylvia's character-book?" persisted Mabs. "You don't mean to say she's let you see it?"

"That's nothing to do with you, either," retorted Rosamund rudely. In her present mood it was a relief to thwart Mabs's unbounded curiosity, and she felt that life was not without its compensations, as she took a short cut up the back stairs to the sanatorium, hoping to restore Sylvia's property before she encountered her form-mistress. But Rosamund's luck was out that evening – at a turn in the upper passage she ran full tilt into Miss Yelland, and her heart sank anew.

"Rosamund! What were you doing across the valley just now? I knew you by your pink dress. And wearing your house shoes, too! Look at them – soaked to pulp! What on earth do you mean by it?"

"Nita Tomlinson sent me," answered Rosamund sulkily.

"Then she had no business to, as you very well know, and you could easily have refused to go," declared Miss Yelland, whose nerves were still suffering from the thunderstorm. "The whole thing was just a piece of naughtiness, and it will be a good thing if it doesn't result in a serious cold. Go straight to bed, and your supper will be sent up to you."

This was a contingency which Rosamund had not fore

seen, and she listened to her sentence with dismay. If Nita made inquiries, and found that her messenger had gone to bed in disgrace, she would probably seek her out in the junior dormitory, and the book would fall into the wrong hands after all. Rosamund, with natural obstinacy, was growing more and more determined that Nita should not get hold of it at any price, and she did the only thing which occurred to her, though startled herself at her own daring.

"Please, then, Miss Yelland," she said, rather more meekly, "will you give this to Sylvia Drummond? It belongs to her, and I was just taking it to the sanitorium when I met you."

She held out the book, and Miss Yelland took it with a careless glance at the covers, still damp and mottled from the rain.

"Very well," she said shortly; and meeting Matron on her way down to supper, she handed it over to her.

"I believe that belongs to your patient," she remarked. "One of the girls gave it to me just now. How is the foot, by the way?"

"Badly swollen," replied Matron, "but it won't take long to put it right if she rests it at once — thanks to that sensible child, Dimsie Maitland."

"I wish they were all as sensible as Dimsie," returned Miss Yelland, relaxing into a smile.

When Matron returned to the sanatorium after supper, she duly restored Sylvia's property to her, saying:

"Miss Yelland asked me to give you this. She says she got it from one of the little ones."

"One of the little ones?" echoed Sylvia in surprise. "Then she must have been out of bounds to get it. Oh, perhaps Dimsie picked it up before I was carried off the scene of action. But this is only my verse-book — I wonder what the kid has done with the other one."

Downstairs, meanwhile, Nita's temper was not improving, as the evening crept on and there was no sign of Rosamund coming to seek her. She began to fear that the book had been taken straight to its rightful owner after all, and in her own mind she uttered dire threats against the disobedient junior who had dared to defy her in this fashion. It was not entirely from idle curiosity that she was so determined to get hold of these character sketches; Nita was a born mischief-maker, as was shown by her past career at Jane's, and she felt that Sylvia's outspoken (or rather, written) comments on their companions would provide her with some useful ammunition against her enemies. Probably some of the studies were quite unflattering enough to endanger the writer's popularity when the subjects came to hear of them, and thus a few of Nita's grievances, against the headgirl at least, would be avenged. She would repeat any caustic remarks she found in the green book under strict secrecy, of course, and each confidante would be left to suppose that Sylvia had shown her scribblings to Nita, which would, if anything, increase the feeling of bitterness which the latter hoped to stir up.

It was a dangerous game, but therein lay part of the fascination to Nita's present frame of mind, and she felt that it would be provoking in the extreme if Rosamund had baulked her of her innocent amusement.

It was nearly bedtime before something occurred which completely mystified her. Daphne Maitland, who had been spending the evening upstairs with her friend, strolled into the senior sitting-room, and exclaimed:

"Oh, there you are, Nita! Sylvia wants to know if you managed to go across for her note-book as you promised, before supper."

"No, I didn't," replied Nita in astonishment. "Hasn't she got it yet? I had to go and see Miss Yelland about that match, but I sent Rosamund Garth to find the book. Do you mean to say she hasn't taken it to Sylvia? I was sure she must have done so, since she hasn't been near me."

"Rosamund Garth?" repeated Daphne. "Oh, that may be the reason then! Rosamund is in disgrace – sent to bed by Miss Yelland for going out of bounds in the damp without boots. So Dimsie has just told me. Listen, Nita, you'd better go and let Miss Yelland know that it was really your fault she went across there. The kid may have thought it was all right when you sent her."

"I shall do no such thing!" retorted Nita spitefully. "It isn't my fault she went without her wellies, the little idiot!

Anyhow, it's past her ordinary bedtime by now, so there's nothing to be gained. But I shall go up and see what she's done with that book."

"I think not," said Daphne coldly. "As you aren't a prefect you can't go into other girls' bedrooms without permission. Besides, there's no need – Primrose or I will go."

Nita cast a malevolent glance after Daphne's departing form, and then turned back to the game of patience she was playing. But her thoughts kept wandering, and she flung the cards across the table in a fit of irritation. Her plans had been thwarted, she realized, and all becuse of that wretched junior. She decided inwardly that Rosamund should be made to suffer for her indiscretions. After all, it was an easy matter to pay off grudges against juniors, even if one had been denied the powers belonging to a prefect. Nita felt that she need scarcely trouble to think out a scheme in this case, for an opportunity was sure to occur before long; but, nevertheless, it was aggravating, for it meant that the pains she had taken to cultivate Rosamund would now be wasted, and she had hoped to make further use of the younger girl's admiration.

# CHAPTER 11

# KEPT IN

Daphne decided to leave Rosamund in peace for that night, but next morning she captured her on her way into breakfast, and inquired:

"What have you done with that note-book of Sylvia's – the one you went to look for last night?"

Rosamund stared up at her in injured surprise. She had come downstairs prepared to face the music with regard to Nita's complaints, but this was a new point of attack.

"Why, I asked Miss Yelland to give it to her, and I thought she was going to. Are you sure she hasn't got it?"

"Quite sure. Miss Yelland did give her one, but not the right one, and I think Sylvia said Dimsie found that."

"It wasn't Dimsie – it was me," replied Rosamund. "I fetched it from where Nita told me to look for it. Isn't it the right one?" she asked anxiously.

"Oh yes, I think so, but there was another as well. You found her poetry book, but she took them both up on to the cliff yesterday afternoon."

"Well, there was only one there," insisted Rosamund, growing more perturbed. "I looked all round, every inch. Honestly, Daphne, I'm certain the other book isn't there. Sylvia must have dreamed that she took two."

Daphne looked perplexed.

"I'll tell her what you say, Rosamund, but I can't understand it. She is quite sure she took them both with her."

Rosamund pondered the question silently while she ate her toast and marmalade. If the book she had found was not the right one, where *was* the right one? Was it possible that Nita herself could have gone out later on and found it, after all? But that question answered itself when Nita seized her arm after prayers and dragged her into an empty classroom.

"What have you done with Sylvia Drummond's notebook, you little beast? I told you to bring it straight to me."

"It wasn't yours," returned Rosamund defiantly. "I gave it to Miss Yelland for Sylvia."

"Yes – one of them," Nita said. "Daphne Maitland told me that. But the other – the one I sent you to fetch – you didn't give that to Miss Yelland."

"I only found one," answered Rosamund sulkily. "I don't know where the other is."

Nita gave her a spiteful little shake.

"Don't tell lies! You know perfectly well where you put it. Go and get it at once."

Rosamund's eyes filled with angry tears.

"I never tell lies, and I haven't the least idea where it is, so there! And if you don't let go my arm at once, I'll scream at the top of my voice!"

Nita dropped her arm, and gave her a violent push which nearly knocked her down.

"I don't believe a word you say, you nasty little worm!" she cried, beside herself with temper. "You wanted to see the book yourself, so you've taken it and hidden it somewhere; but this isn't the last you're going to hear of it, not by a long shot!"

Rosamund escaped and dashed upstairs to the dormitory, where she had scarcely time to make her bed before the big bell clanged above for morning school, and everybody ran off to their classrooms. Rosamund hurried down, to receive an order-mark for being late; and her heart sank again as she slipped into her seat, for the first lesson was history, and Dimsie had not heard her dates the previous afternoon, owing to the fact that Nita's photographs had needed to be developed in the hour after tea.

Poor Rosamund acquitted herself badly in school that morning, and the climax came when her form-mistress remarked sharply that, if this sort of thing continued, she saw no prospect of any moving up for at least another term. When the others were released at twelve o'clock, Rosamund stayed behind with a wearisome long-division sum which would not come right.

"Hey! Are you being kept in?"

Dimsie's head appeared at the open window framed in a picturesque setting of purple clematis. As the Third Form room was on the upper floor of the schoolroom buildings. Rosamund beheld the apparition with very natural astonishment.

"However did you get up there?" she inquired.

Dimsie swung herself carefully in over the sill and dropped, feet first, on the polished wooden floor boards.

"It's quite easy," she answered jauntily. "I'm surprised none of us thought of it before. You just go up the creeper like a ladder, and there you are."

"It was an awfully dangerous thing to do," declared Rosamund, but with no thought for the bodily risk, as her next words proved. "Suppose Miss Yelland had been up here with me!"

"I knew she wasn't," returned Dimsie. "I watched her go down to the playing field with the second eleven, and then I came up here, 'cause Nora Blyth told me you'd had to stay behind."

"It's this sum," said Rosamund hopelessly. "I can't get it right; and, oh, Dimsie! My lessons have been so bad lately that Miss Yelland says she doesn't believe I'll be moved up for years and years!"

"Well, don't cry," said Dimsie kindly, putting her arm round the shaking shoulders. "It's only because you haven't had any help for about a fortnight. You really must chuck this Nita business, and let me hear your prep after tea, as I did before."

"If she tells me to do things, have I got to?" asked Rosamund dejectedly. "She's a Sixth Former, you know."

"Not if you don't want to, you little nutcase! Not things like that, anyhow. I mean, if Daph or Joyce, or even Sylvia, wanted us to run around for them like that, they'd only ask us as a favour – they wouldn't *make* us do things – and they're prefects."

"They're quite different from Nita Tomlinson, though," Rosamund pointed out, with a little sniff.

Dimsie's face lighted up eagerly.

"Do you mean to say you don't like her any more?" she demanded.

"No, I don't," said Rosamund with emphasis. "I very nearly hate her, only not quite, because I suppose that's a very wicked thing to do, so I'd better not."

"But – but you were always hanging round her up till yesterday," said Dimsie bluntly. "Erica and the others are awfully sick with you about it. They think you've got like Joan and Betty and Winnie, and they want to turn you out of the Anti-Soppists."

"I knew they would," said Rosamund, choking back a sob, "and I didn't mind so much while I was getting on with Nita; but I've been getting rather tired of her for about three days, and then yesterday I found out she was very horrid, so I don't want to have anything more to do with her."

And she told Dimsie the story of last night's happenings, and the mysterious disappearance of the note-book which Nita had been so anxious to get hold of.

"What do you think she wanted it for?" asked Rosamund. "It couldn't have been just curiosity, or she wouldn't have got into such a frightful rage about it."

"I don't know," said Dimsie, knitting her brows thoughtfully. "I always feel that you can never quite tell why Nita does things. But I wonder where Sylvia's book is."

"I don't know," said Rosamund. "Dimsie, do you think Erica and all of you will have me back again now that I've given up being gone on Nita?"

"Oh, I think so," replied Dimsie readily. "At least, if you promise not to do anything like that again. Now, let's see if I can help you with this sum, and then we can go and tell Erica. What is it? Long division? Oh, that's not hard!"

Rosamund's brains revived with her reviving spirits, and in a very short time the sum was worked out correctly, ready to be given in to Miss Yelland after dinner. The two girls ran downstairs and out into the grounds in search of their companions, whom Dimsie believed to be down in the playing field practising at the nets, for the Lower Fourth were becoming increasingly keen on cricket. Halfway down the wood path, however, they met a Middle School girl, who pounced on Rosamund with relief.

"Where in the world have you been?" she asked indignantly. "I've searched the whole of Jane's for you! Sylvia Drummond says you're to go to her at once. She's lying out on a sunbed under the big cedar. I think it's about some book of hers that you've been and lost."

"All right," said Rosamund, her voice beginning to shake again; "but I haven't lost it."

She turned back towards the upper garden, pulling Dimsie after her.

"If Sylvia's in a rage with me, I can't go alone," she whimpered. "Do you suppose Nita's been telling her I've got the book all the time? That was what she said to me."

"I shouldn't be a bit surprised," said Dimsie cheerfully; "but you needn't worry about that. Sylvia knows better than to listen to Nita Tomlinson. I expect she just wants to know if you looked everywhere for it last night, because, of course, she won't like to think it's lying about for anybody to pick up and read. I heard her talking to Daphne about it, when she stayed with us last holidays, and I know she has written down just what she thinks about lots of the girls. You can see for yourself that it wouldn't do for just anybody to read a book like that; they might get awfully mad with Sylvia. She said she always took jolly good care not to leave it about."

# CHAPTER 12

# UNDER SUSPICION

Sylvia had hobbled down to the schoolroom after breakfast that morning, and had done her usual work lying on the old couch in the corner. When twelve o'clock came, the girls had carried the patient out into the shade of the big cedar, where Matron decreed she was to pass the rest of the day, having her meals brought out to her. Here Nita found her, strolling up with her racket in her hand.

"Oh, Sylvia, about your book," she began, with one of her sharp, covert glances. "Did Daphne tell you that I sent Rosamund Garth for it? It seems she only brought back one, and that it's the wrong one."

"Why the wrong one?" queried Sylvia lazily. "I was very glad to get that one back, anyhow."

"Yes," said Nita, stammering a little, "but there was another – at least, Daphne said . . ."

"There certainly was," Sylvia rejoined, "but apparently Rosamund couldn't find it, for the simple reason that it wasn't there. Primrose has just been across and had a thorough good search."

Nita came closer, and dropped her voice to confidential tones.

"I shouldn't be so sure of that," she said significantly. "That Rosamund couldn't find it, I mean. It seems to me that child is hiding something. I've been asking her about it and I believe she knows where it is."

Sylvia's languid grey eyes suddenly opened wide.

"Why?" she asked shortly.

"Oh, well! Rosamund was remarkably anxious to read

that book, as any of her little pals will tell you – and I thought her manner was very suspicious this morning."

"H'm!" said Sylvia. "I'd better judge that for myself. Hoy, Madge!"

A Lower Sixth girl, who was passing at that moment, came across the grass in answer to her call.

"Yes, Sylvia? Can I fetch anything for you?"

"Yes, please, if it's not too much trouble. I want to speak to Rosamund Garth. She's probably down at the nets with the other juniors."

Madge Anderson ran off, and Nita lingered long enough to say:

"I'm afraid you'll find her rather a bore to deal with. She strikes me as being rather an untruthful kid."

"Do you think so?" asked Sylvia coldly. "I always find our juniors a very straightforward lot. Don't let me keep you from your tennis. I see they are waiting for a fourth on that court."

Nita departed, leaving Sylvia to wonder what Rosamund could have done to offend the games-captain to such an extent.

"I should hardly have thought she'd take the trouble to harbour malice against such a mite!" mused the headgirl scornfully. "At any rate, I don't think Primrose need concern herself over that alliance much more. I suspect it must be pretty well at an end."

She had some time to wait for the result of her message. Nearly twenty minutes passed before Rosamund appeared, accompanied by Dimsie Maitland. Sylvia, who had paid no attention to Nita's insinuations, was astonished to see how scared and guilty the junior looked, and that she hung back nervously behind Dimsie, as though afraid of being questioned.

"What's the matter with you, Rosamund?" Sylvia asked, holding out her hand. "I only want to inquire about my note-book . . ."

"Please, Sylvia, I never even saw it!" broke in Rosamund in frightened tones. "I'm sure it wasn't there, but if I had found it, I'd have given it to Miss Yelland with the other. I wouldn't have done such a thing, no matter how much I wanted to read it!"

Sylvia eyed her sharply.

"Don't be a little twit! I haven't suggested yet that you did anything at all. I only wanted to find out . . ."

"There isn't anything to find out," protested Rosamund hurriedly, but Dimsie pulled her up with a little shake.

"Don't go on like that, Ros, or Sylvia'll think you've got her book hidden away somewhere," she exclaimed. "Shut up, and listen to what she's going to say!"

"Quite right, Dimsie!" rejoined Sylvia drily. "I *was* beginning to think that Rosamund 'doth protest too much', if you know what that means. Now, Rosamund, I'm merely trying to ask you whether you might possibly have dropped the other book on your way back?"

"No," said Rosamund, calming down slightly. "I never had more than one, Sylvia – really I hadn't."

Sylvia looked at her silently for a moment then she said:

"All right, I believe you, so you needn't worry any more. But I wish to goodness I knew where that book had got to! Never mind, it's not your fault, and Primrose has hunted the whole neighbourhood this morning, so it's no use sending you back to search again. Run away and play, both of you."

She turned back to her magazine, and the two juniors, finding themselves dismissed, went slowly and silently together through the shrubbery. Rosamund had sunk back into gloom, and Dimsie's active brain was occupied with possible solutions of the mystery, till a sniff from her friend brought her attention back to present happenings.

"Whatever is the matter now?" she asked patiently.

"Sylvia s-said she believed me," replied Rosamund, "but I don't s-suppose anybody else will, and I shan't feel my name's been cleared till that h-horrid thing is found."

"Oh, don't be so daft!" cried Dimsie with vigour. "Why shouldn't everybody believe you? You know, Rosamund, though I should never think of calling you soppy, you do get some weird ideas into your head, and I'm not surprised that Erica and the rest laugh at you sometimes."

"I know," said Rosamund humbly, "but this isn't an idea in my head exactly, for Nita did say I hadn't heard the last of it."

The dinner gong rang before they could find their companions, and after that came preparation, followed by tea, so that it was not until their cricket practice was over that Erica and her band of five gathered once more at the tennis courts, where they sat in a group on the grass discussing the prospects for next Saturday's tournament. Then, to her surprise, Dimsie found that Rosamund had been right in her forebodings.

"I meant to call a meeting about you in the council chamber, Ros," said Erica without preamble, "but since we're all here, I don't see why we need move. Did you know that half of Jane's is saying you've got Sylvia's book stowed away somewhere, and won't give it up?"

"I never heard such a load of codswallop!" burst out Dimsie angrily. "And you ought to be ashamed of yourself, Erica Innes, for listening to it! Is it likely any of *us* would do a thing like that?"

"Well, I shouldn't have thought so once," answered Erica, holding her ground, "but Rosamund hasn't been an Anti-Soppist just lately, and she has been running round after Nita Tomlinson."

"You can't blame people for believing things of anyone who's running after Nita Tomlinson," argued Jean.

"But I'm not!" cried Rosamund vehemently. "Honestly I'm not, Erica! I stopped liking her last night, when I found out how mean she could be, and I do want to be a proper Anti-Soppist again. And – and I never even *saw* that book! It was the other one I found and gave to Miss Yelland."

"But Margaret Hunter told Mabs at teatime that everyone is quite sure you've got it, and have kept it back to read, and now you're afraid to confess, and so . . ."

Dimsie rose determinedly to her feet.

"Of course Margaret's too big for me," she said in an ominous tone, "but I've fought Mabs before, and I'll fight her again for daring to pay any attention to such a story about Rosamund."

But Mabs was also on her feet, and had bolted for cover to the rhododendron bushes, while Erica clutched Dimsie's skirt firmly from behind.

"No, you don't!" she said. "Mabs didn't make it up, so you needn't go on as though she had. Besides, we're all quite

willing to take Rosamund's word for it, if she'll swear she really
has dumped that awful Nita."

"Of course she has!" retorted Dimsie, still heated. "Hurry
up and swear it, Rosamund!"

"Honest and true,
Black and blue,
Lay me down and cut me in two!"

chanted Rosamund obediently. "Now will you believe me
about that book?"

"All right – we will," said Erica. "We're bound to, when
you've taken your oath. And of course we'll make everyone else
believe it, too. You can come back, Mabs – it's quite safe.
Dimsie doesn't want to fight you any more."

"I wasn't afraid," explained Mabs carefully, as she returned to the circle on the grass, "but you know what Dimsie is
– she never stops to think when she's in a rage, and Miss
Yelland was just looking our way. Besides, it would have put the
tennis players off so frightfully if there'd been a fight just behind
them."

"You *were* afraid," returned Dimsie amiably, "but it's all
right now. The rest of you are all going to believe in Rosamund,
so I needn't fight anybody – at least, not any of us lot."

"But I shall still feel there's a stain on my character,"
persisted Rosamund, "until that green note-book of Sylvia's is
found."

"Oh, well, then," said Dimsie loyally, "I suppose I shall
just have to find it somehow. Anyway, you can stop crying in
the meantime, which is something."

# CHAPTER 13

# THE DOUBLES CHAMPIONSHIP

Saturday afternoon arrived, bright and still, an ideal day for a tennis tournament on shady courts such as those at the Jane Willard, and the six couples who were to contend for the championship strolled across the terrace, outwardly cool in their neat white dresses, but inwardly extremely nervous.

"It's this horrible new scheme of Miss Yorke's that's putting me off," groaned Meg Flynn. "This is the first time the public's been admitted to watch our struggles."

"I know," agreed Daisy Milne miserably. "Look at the crowds of people in chairs under the trees over there!"

"Crowds of people!" laughed Daphne Maitland, who had been forced to "scratch" owing to her partner's accident, and could afford to regard the visitors with an untroubled spirit. "Anyone would think there was a hundred at least, to listen to you! There are no more than a dozen people there all told – outsiders, I mean – the rest are teachers and non-combatants."

"Even a dozen outsiders are upsetting," persisted Daisy. "I can't imagine what Miss Yorke was thinking about!"

"Well, I can," broke in Miss Yelland briskly, as she followed them down the grass slope from the terrace. "If you and your partner win the tournament you will have to play before several dozen strangers at different matches. This afternoon is to decide our champions for the season, and Miss Yorke wants to test you under fire, so to speak."

"Well, it only makes victory more certain for Meg and Nita, since they are the coolest couple of the lot."

"Nonsense! That remains to be seen. Now, come along. Daisy and Joyce in this court against Nell and Ursula . . ."

Miss Yelland rapidly made her arrangements, and started the two opening sets, while Daphne retreated to her partner's sunbed beside the rhododendrons, where they had a good view of the courts.

"Are you absolutely mad at missing it?" she asked sympathetically, but Sylvia shook her fair head.

"We might have beaten some of the others, but we hadn't a chance against Meg and Nita. They've spent every spare moment practising. You've won the singles, Daph – let that content you."

"It must," laughed Daphne. "Look, Sylvia! there's that Miss Austin from the St Elstrith Club. You know, they challenged us, both singles and doubles, and Miss Yorke declined."

"Why?" asked Sylvia idly. "We used to play them in Miss Darrel's time."

(For Miss Yorke had only succeeded Miss Darrel as headmistress of Jane's at the beginning of the previous autumn term.)

"Miss Yelland says the club has gone down badly. She played there once last month, and they've got a lot of new members who are very rowdy and unpleasant. I really think it was she who put Miss Yorke up to refusing their challenge."

Sylvia lay in silence for a short while, watching the play, which so far had not been very exciting. The girls were still nervous, and painfully conscious of the "outsiders".

"I didn't know that was her reason for refusing," she said presently, going back to the subject, "but I knew Nita was terribly annoyed about it. The only thing that girl cares about besides herself is that Jane's should do well at sport, and her heart was set on beating the St Elstrith Club."

"I know," assented Daphne. "It *is* hard luck, for they've got a name for tennis, and they always beat us in the past. Remember what a thrashing I got from their champion in the singles last summer?"

Sylvia nodded.

"I believe Nita's dying to wipe out that defeat, but it can't be helped. Oh, look! That four have finished! Dimsie, make yourself useful, go and find out their scores."

Dimsie, who had been sitting on the ground beside them,

intent on the play, scampered off willingly. She returned quickly with the information that Nell Anderson and Ursula Grey had beaten their opponents, and were to meet Meg and Nita next in the other court.

"They're good, that pair," said Daphne critically. "They play well together, but they can't stand up to Meg and Nita. The next set ought to be worth seeing."

"They might win," argued her small cousin. "They beat Joyce and Daisy six-two, and that'll help their total a lot."

"They might," Sylvia agreed. "Stranger things have happened in a tournament. Hey, Daph, suppose Nita gets knocked out altogether!"

Daphne laughed.

"She'd hate it, of course; but I'll say this for Nita – she always wants the best person to play for her side, even if she's not the best person herself. However, she generally is. Her nerves are always steady, which is a great help."

"There they go!" exclaimed Daphne. "They've won the toss – oh, they're taking service! Quite right. Meg's serve is most intimidating to her opponents."

Meg Flynn's strong serve had a curious spin in it, from which Jane's hoped great things. Even her school-fellows, accustomed to playing against her, went down before that spin, and it was felt that it would be invincible against strangers. Ursula Grey stood up to it gallantly, and scored two points; but Nell was nervous, and sent all her returns out. The first game was won by Meg and Nita, and Ursula prepared to serve.

Knowing that those couples were the strongest, the rest of the school watched with an eagerness which scarcely heeded the less interesting set in the neighbouring court. The Upper Fifth, to which form Nell and Ursula belonged, were loudly clapping every point which their pair contrived to score. "After all," as one of them said, "our two beat Meg and Nita, when the Sixth Form played the Fifth Form."

"That was a fortnight ago," her companion pointed out grimly. "They won't do it again if Nita can help it, and you can see Meg's taking it a lot more seriously today."

The Irish girl seemed, indeed, to be all over the court at once, depending largely on the brilliance of her play, for she had not much staying power. Nita, on the other hand, held on to every rally, and frequently won it by her tireless obstinacy. She and Meg made an excellent combination.

"Two all!" exclaimed Daphne. "Wow! It's pretty close, Sylvia. Nell has pulled herself together now. Look at that! Oh, brilliant! Well placed, Ursula!"

"Ursula goes in for placing," observed Sylvia "but her strokes are not as strong as Nita's."

It was Meg's serve next, and she fired her balls across with redoubled vigour. The other side returned them once or twice, only to receive them back again in a fierce rally, mostly from Nita. Ursula, who was something of a strategist, tried to direct her shots at Meg, but failed. Amid groans from the Upper Fifth the elder pair scored a love game.

"Meg and Nita seem to grow stronger every minute!" exclaimed Daphne. "And Nell's weakening again. She – she sent that ball right out, and it wasn't a hard one to take. Oh, good shot Nita! Right down the tramlines!"

"Five-two!" called the umpire from her chair. The other four had finished their set, and Miss Yelland was busily marking up their score on the blackboard; but no one paid any attention. School and visitors alike hung on the game just opening with Nita's serve. Would it be decisive, or was there still a flicker of hope for the Middle School girls? For five minutes, perhaps, the result hung in the balance; then Ursula took the fatal step forward to play net. Seeing her opportunity, Nita buzzed her returns hard at her, and Meg instantly followed suit. Ursula made heroic efforts to stop them, but the balls were so fast that those she succeeded in touching flew far out. Amid tremendous cheers and applause came the umpire's shout of "Game and . . ."

Primrose Garth had watched her friend's triumph from the background of the spectators, and now pressed forward with congratulations.

"That was brilliant, Meg!" she cried, as the victors stepped back into the crowd after receiving Miss Yorke's hearty praise. "You and Nita work fantastically well together. You ought to pull off lots of matches for Jane's."

Meg turned, looking a trifle dazed by the success and the

loud clapping of her school-fellows.

"Sure, Nita's splendid!" she cried, her brogue deepening, as it always did, with excitement. "I couldn't have done half as well without her. Thanks, Primrose – yes, I hope we can keep it up; but we haven't won the tournament yet, you know."

"Oh, you will, easily! Come and have tea with me," begged Primrose wistfully. "The other sets aren't being played till afterwards."

Meg glanced at her half absently, then moved off in response to a hail from her partner.

"Sorry," she said. "I promised Nita. Didn't you know? Don't keep me now – she's waving to me. I tell you there isn't a better player in the school than Nita Tomlinson!"

# CHAPTER 14

# A CHALLENGE

The rest of the tournament was something of an anti-climax. It was obvious that Meg and Nita must win, and interest centred entirely on their matches, till they defeated the last of the couples whom they had still to meet, and left the remaining encounters to be played off.

"We've got it!" said Meg, with a little sigh, as she scanned the figures on the blackboard. "Those who are still in it can't touch our sum-total now, however hard they try."

"Of course not," assented Nita complacently. "Personally, I hadn't a doubt, but tournaments do take queer turns sometimes. Look, Meg! There's Miss Austin beckoning to us. You know her, don't you? She's secretary to the tennis club at St Elstrith."

"Yes, I know. She often comes to watch our matches. I wonder what she thinks about Miss Yorke's refusal to let us play them."

Nita's face darkened into its most unprepossessing scowl.

"I know what *I* think! But, unfortunately, that's another matter."

Apparently Miss Austin bore no grudge for the snub administered by the headmistress of Jane's. She was one of those elderly young ladies, harmless except for a tendency to gush, who are not, as a rule, popular with schoolgirls. Nita, however, liked her, and enjoyed her exaggerated praise of the school's prowess in all games, and especially in tennis.

"Your partner's serve was wonderful, dear – quite wonderful! We have no one at St Elstrith who can touch it – or even touch the balls she sends, and that's the most important thing, isn't it?" She threw an arch glance at the embarrassed Meg. "Now, tell me why you're not playing us this season? Our champions would love to meet you."

Meg discreetly held her tongue, and left the answer to Nita, who gave it glibly enough.

"Miss Yorke doesn't care for us to play more than a certain number of matches in the term, and our fixture card was full when your challenge came."

"So she told me, but surely a point might be stretched in favour of such old enemies? I must talk to her again. Why not next Saturday, for example? Is next Saturday full?"

A curious, eager expression crossed Nita's face.

"Not for us," she responded. "The second eleven from Earnswood are playing our second here, but, of course, that has nothing to do with Meg or myself."

Meg, who saw where this reply was likely to lead, opened her lips hurriedly, but Nita, whose arm was linked in hers, pinched her fiercely, and Miss Austin exclaimed:

"Then why shouldn't you meet two of us on that day? Not a regular match of course, dears, since Miss Yorke is apparently inclined to be – shall I say – a tiny bit fussy? Just a friendly encounter to let us see what the best players at the Jane Willard can do when they take on a good club. And your champion for the singles, too – Dorothy Maitland, isn't it? – perhaps she would come with you, and give me a set? You know," with a visible preening, "I usually play for my club in singles."

"I know, but I'm afraid that wouldn't do – about Daphne Maitland, I mean," replied Nita hastily. "She's – she's – I think she's busy next Saturday. I don't know why we shouldn't play though, eh, Meg?"

"Indeed, and I'd be delighted," returned Meg with obvious longing, "but Miss Yorke may not let us."

"I'll go and tackle her now," declared Miss Austin, preparing to bustle off, but Nita interposed in some alarm:

"No, I shouldn't, Miss Austin! Please don't – not just now. If you'll be good enough to leave it to me, I'll ask her later, and let you know. That will be all right, won't it?"

"Oh, certainly, dear! You want to get your school-marm in a good temper – that's it, isn't it? Very well, manage it your own way, but you simply *must* play us! Such style and finish I haven't seen, even at the Jane Willard before! Cheerio, girls! I must find Miss Yorke now and thank her for my pleasant afternoon."

She rustled off across the grass, leaving the two girls alone for a few minutes, and Meg caught hold of her friend's arm excitedly.

"Do you suppose Miss Yorke will let us go, Nita? Such a thing never happened before in the memory of man!"

"You leave it to me," responded Nita, with a mysterious little nod. "And listen, Meg, don't go chattering about it to the others. I'm sure I shall get permission from Miss Yorke, but she won't want it to become a precedent, and I'd better be able to tell her that we haven't talked about it to the rest, and don't mean to – see?"

"Sure I do," said Meg readily enough. "She couldn't be giving the whole school exeats to play informal matches at tennis clubs. I only hope you manage to talk her round – it would be great if we could beat them."

"Naturally we'll beat them," declared Nita, thrusting out her chin determinedly. "Oh boy – this'll be a *real* game of tennis!"

For two days nothing more was said about Miss Austin's challenge, then Nita pulled Meg back as the Sixth Form trooped out of their classroom after morning school on Tuesday.

"See that?" she queried triumphantly, holding up a letter addressed to the Secretary of the St Elstrith Tennis Club.

"Great!" cried Meg delightedly. "Then you've got permission? Somehow, I never thought Miss Yorke would let us, though you seemed so sure you could persuade her. What did she say, Nita?"

"Oh, nothing really," returned Nita, reddening a little under her sallow skin. "But, listen, Meg! Don't mention this to a soul – and above all, don't refer to it if you go up to see Miss Yorke about anything between now and Saturday. She might take it into her head to forbid us after all, you know."

Meg felt that this was not altogether improbable.

"Better not to remind her of the subject," she agreed,

laughing. "We can easily slip away without any flourish of trumpets on Saturday afternoon."

"Exactly," assented Nita. "Well, I must be off with this if I'm to catch the mid-day post."

She ran off through the shrubbery in the direction of the school gates, and Meg wandered through the wood, supposing that, with the permission to write the note, Miss Yorke had given leave to post it. Ordinarily, all letters going out from the Jane Willard had to be put into the post-box in the hall, from which they were collected and taken up to the headmistress, who scrutinized the addresses before allowing them to pass.

Half unconsciously Meg's feet strayed into a path which was little frequented, and she found herself at the old twisted cedar which had been a favourite haunt of hers and Primrose's in the previous summer terms, before Meg's love of sport had brought her so much under the influence of Nita Tomlinson. To her surprise, Primrose was there now, perched on the lowest branch, and leaning back listlessly against the mossy trunk. She looked round with a start at the sound of Meg's step on the crisp dry needles, and the colour rose in her face.

"Oh, Meg!" she exclaimed eagerly. "Were you looking for me? Come and sit down. It's so nice and cool in our old hidey-hole."

With Irish tact Meg refrained from telling her that she had wandered there quite by accident, and swinging herself onto a higher branch opposite, she said:

"I must tell you something, Primrose – only it's meant to be a secret. Promise you won't breathe a word to a soul!"

"Of course not!" cried Primrose, delighted to be once more the recipient of any secret of Meg's.

The other girl leaned towards her and lowered her voice confidentially.

"You know that Miss Austin person from St Elstrith who came to our tournament on Saturday? Well, she was rather put out that Jane's wasn't playing that club of theirs this term, and guess what! She's asked Nita and me to meet their champions quite privately – just us two – next Saturday, and Nita got Miss Yorke to say we could!"

Primrose looked her astonishment.

"Well, you're jolly lucky, then, Meg. I'm positive no one's been allowed to do anything like that before. Isn't she even going to send a mistress with you?"

Meg tossed her red head rather defiantly.

"She never said anything about it, but I shouldn't think so. I'm a prefect, even if Nita isn't, and it's only a mile to the village."

"Oh, I know," said Primrose, "but there will be such a lot of grown-ups when you get there."

"Really, Primrose, we do occasionally mix with grown-ups in the holidays! That old-fashioned boarding-school idea of shutting us up like nuns in a convent is absurd nowadays. Even Miss Yorke goes in far too much for it."

Primrose recognized this as an opinion of Nita's.

"I suppose school has to be school, all the same," she observed sagely, "and holidays are holidays – otherwise they wouldn't be such a treat. But don't let's waste time arguing. Tell me, are you nervous at the thought of playing all those other schools which have challenged us?"

"Not a bit!" declared Meg gaily. "No one could be with a partner like Nita. It gives one confidence to play with her. Have you noticed that curious serve of hers, Primrose?"

She launched into an enthusiastic description of Nita's play, to which Primrose listened wearily, anxious to cloak her lack of interest with a show of sympathy rather than run the risk of losing her friend's resumed confidences. She asked intelligent questions at the right moment, and Meg prattled happily on, much too absorbed in her subject to notice that Primrose looked pale and jaded. They went up to dinner arm in arm when the bell rang, and though Meg ran off almost immediately in search of Nita, Primrose felt more cheerful than she had done since the beginning of the term, for Meg had sought her out and confided in her as she used to do in the days before Nita's ascendancy.

# CHAPTER 15

# PRIMROSE
# FALLS SICK

"This is dreadfully bad luck, Nita – the match with Westover High School seems fated!" exclaimed the games-mistress, coming into the Sixth Form room shortly before tea on the following Monday afternoon.

"Why? What's happened, Miss Yelland?" inquired several anxious voices, as the owners looked up from their desks.

"Haven't you heard about Primrose Garth?" responded Miss Yelland. "She's been sent over to hospital with influenza! I met Matron just now on her way back from seeing the doctor off the premises."

There was a chorus of dismay, and Meg Flynn exclaimed:

"She was awfully low this morning, and Daphne fetched Matron for her, but none of us dreamed it was as bad as that."

"Well, I'm afraid it is," said Miss Yelland gloomily. "First Sylvia's foot, and now this! Sylvia, at least, will be able to bat, but we'll have to find a substitute for Primrose from the second eleven."

"I suppose it will have to be Tony Semple, then," said Nita. "Don't you think so, Miss Yelland? Her batting is nowhere near as good as Primrose's, but can you suggest anyone more suitable?"

"No," replied Miss Yelland. "I don't believe I can; but let me tell you, girls, it will take you all your time to win that match now! Not a bad thing, perhaps, for everyone will be on her mettle. And, Nita, there's another matter which mustn't be overlooked, and you, as captain of games, are the proper person to attend to it. I suppose you know that the juniors have challenged the Middle School?''

Nita laughed rather scornfully.

"Isn't it absurd?'' she said. "But I daresay it wouldn't do to disappoint the kids. Okay, Miss Yelland, I'll see to it. I shall have to go down and watch their play tonight, and pick an eleven.''

"Primrose has done that already,'' observed Joyce Lamond, looking up from her French exercise. "She drew up the list last night and gave it to me to print off for the hall notice board. I was just going to put it up after tea.''

"Very well, Joyce; do so, then,'' said Miss Yelland. "It's a good thing that list was made,'' she added to Nita. "Primrose has coached those children untiringly, and she can judge of their play better than either you or I.''

"Really,'' said Nita languidly, "the match is not of very great importance, is it, Miss Yelland? But, of course I will go down and watch the juniors tonight, and give them a few hints.''

The games-mistress turned away with an exasperated gesture.

"Any school match is of importance,'' she answered sharply, "and you shouldn't need me to tell you that! The affairs of the Lower School are as interesting to them as yours are to you. Give me that list, Joyce. I'll put it up as I go through the hall.''

Nita flushed, for snubs were something she particularly resented.

"I forgot,'' she remarked indulgently, as the door closed, "that Miss Yelland is the Third Form's form-mistress. Perhaps I was a little tactless.''

"Oh, no!'' rejoined Joyce, who could never resist the temptation to try her shafts of sarcasm on Nita's hardened skin. "I really think it was Miss Yelland who was tactless.''

Nita stared at her suspiciously, and then turned back to her work.

"Of course,'' she said finally, "if I consider that the list requires alteration, I shan't hesitate to make it.''

Meanwhile the said list came in for a good deal of attention as the school crowded through the hall on its way to tea.

Jean Gordon had been chosen captain, but that had been long foreseen by her special circle and called for less comment in consequence.

"Eric's in it! And Pam, and Joan!" shrilled Mabs Hunter, hopping round with one foot in her hand, as was her habit in moments of emotion.

"And good old Rosamund, too! Ros, do you know you're in our eleven? That's your over-arm bowling that you've been practising so hard."

Rosamund's pretty little face went pink with pleasure. She had tried very hard to get into the junior eleven, for at home they were a cricketing family, and she had been trained to bowl overarm ever since she could throw a ball at all. Lately, however, a fear had crept over her lest Primrose should consider it necessary to set her aside because of their relationship, and she had been prepared for disappointment when the list went up. But Primrose knew her little sister's value to the team better than to do anything so foolish.

"When is the match?" Rosamund asked eagerly. "Saturday week? Oh, Mabs, do you think we shall beat them? We must practise frantically hard."

Neither Mabs herself nor Dimsie were among the fortunate ones, but they were much too delighted at the success of their friends to be long crestfallen. After all, hadn't one of the Anti-Soppists been chosen captain of the team?

"I really think I'd rather have you in it than me," Dimsie confided to Rosamund. "I'd be awfully nervous, and drop catches, and do all sorts of idiotic things."

"But so shall I," protested Rosamund, "especially this evening, if Nita comes down to watch us, as Jean says she's going to."

"Nonsense!" said Dimsie. "You'll just have to play all the harder. Who cares about Nita, even if she *is* captain of games?"

Nevertheless, she watched her friend anxiously later on, when Jean led her picked eleven against the remainder of the juniors. Dimsie had taken Rosamund completely under her wing this term, and already things had gone wrong once or twice. Since the break with Nita, however, lessons had improved and marks gone up correspondingly, so there was now every hope that Miss Yelland would give a good report to Miss Yorke at half-term – when the great match, Juniors *v.* Middle School, had been fixed.

"If only Rosamund could make a big score or do the hat trick," thought Dimsie, "and get moved up, all in one day – oh, that would really cheer her up!"

The juniors found it pretty nerve-racking to be critically watched by Nita Tomlinson, but Jean, who had the makings of a great leader, found a way to brace her team.

"She thinks we can't play!" she snorted, as she led them out to battle. "She's always made fun of us and sneered at Primrose, so now we'll jolly well show her what we can do! Pam, you bowl first, and Betty, keep wicket . . ."

She arranged her field with a coolness which gave the flutterers courage, and play commenced. Dimsie, who was batting on the other side, watched eagerly while she awaited her turn to go in. It was difficult to play one's best when one was anxious that one's opponents might give a good account of themselves, and our heroine had only four runs to her credit when she retired; but she looked as delighted as though she had scored a century.

"Terrific the way Rosamund held that!" she declared. "Wasn't it, Joan? And just wait till she goes on to bowl!"

Rosamund certainly acquitted herself very well before stumps were drawn at supper-time, and Jean thumped her warmly on the back as they all trooped up together through the larches.

"Keep it up, Ros!" she adjured her. "Train your eye a bit before the match comes off so as not to bowl wides – that's all I ask of you."

"I know I bowled two wides tonight," confessed Rosamund seriously, "and you know, Jean, it's horribly hard not to go on doing it when once you start."

"That's why you mustn't start, then," returned Jean promptly. "Grief! There's the bell! Come on, you others – I'll race you across the tennis courts."

One or two of the seniors gathered on the terrace after supper that evening to discuss the prospects of "the Babes' Match", as Nita persisted in calling it.

"They didn't do so badly, though," she admitted. "That kid Jean will be quite good some day, and Pamela Hughes can bowl, after a fashion."

"She's awfully slow, though," commented Phyllis Heathley. "Rosamund Garth is much their best bowler."

"I don't agree with you," said Nita sharply, looking up from a paper on which she was scribbling as she sat on the low stone balustrade "What's the use of bowling overarm if you send down wides? Pamela and Winnie are much more reliable."

"Be fair, Nita!" protested Phyllis, warming to her argument. "The kid was nervous."

"Exactly – she isn't reliable. If she was nervous tonight, what would she be like in the match?"

"Ever so much better," returned Phyllis promptly. "Those nervous people always pull themselves together when anything is really depending on them. Besides, Winnie Hatton dropped a catch."

"And Pamela ran Betty out," added Meg Flynn. "Really, Nita, they're not a patch on that little Rosamund. She'll be a regular sportswoman one of these days."

Nita's face took on its dourest expression.

"Oh, of course – she's Primrose Garth's sister!" she returned, with a disagreeable sneer. "But, all the same, I don't agree with you, Meg, or Phyllis, and I might as well tell you I've made up my mind to cross Rosamund off the list. I'm going to play Dimsie Maitland instead."

# CHAPTER 16

# ROSAMUND
# THE MISFORTUNATE

"Have you heard? Have you heard? A perfectly terrible thing has happened!"

Mabs Hunter broke in upon the Anti-Soppists in conclave in the tool shed, her face red, her eyes round and staring with dismay.

"What? What?" cried the other five in chorus. "Don't beat about the bush, Mabs, if it's anything serious – tell us quickly!"

But Mabs was too genuinely upset to need any urging this time.

"It's that beast Nita again!" she cried incoherently. "She's struck off poor old Rosamund's name from the list in the hall, and she's put on Dimsie Maitland's instead!"

"She's what?" Dimsie was on her feet in a moment, knocking over her flowerpot with a swirl of her skirt which smashed it to atoms. "Does she think she's going to put me in Rosamund's place? I'll tell her what I think of it – I shan't play – I . . ."

Erica clutched her firmly from behind.

"Now, don't fly into one of your dancing-mad rages! You know you always scare Mabs, and then we can get nothing out of her. It's all right, Mabs – she shan't touch you, and it isn't your fault, anyhow. But are you quite sure? Who told you?"

"I saw it myself on the notice board, and somebody said it was because Rosamund bowled two wides; but I believe it's just because she'd the sense to stop being soppy over Nita."

"That's it, of course," agreed Pamela. "Beastly rotten cow! She's doing it to pay poor old Ros back."

Here Rosamund, who had listened in silent horror to this

shattering of all her hopes, dissolved into tears, and Jean wailed:

"But we'll lose the match for certain! Nobody can bowl like Rosamund, and Dimsie can't even throw straight."

"You needn't worry," exploded Dimsie afresh, "for I don't even mean to try, so there! There's no use her sticking my name down, for I'm not going to play!"

"B-but Nita will make you," sobbed Rosamund.

"No she won't," returned Dimsie darkly. "You can take a horse to the water, but you can't make it bowl, and I shall go and tell her so at once."

She switched her dress out of Erica's grasp, and was off before they could stop her. They saw her through the open doorway dashing headlong up the slope between the fir trees, till she vanished among the rhododendrons above.

"That's the thing about Dimsie," sighed Erica. "She's so slap-dash! Now she'll go and offend Nita, and I bet our match will be squashed. Nita is just longing for an excuse."

"She can't," said Pamela decidedly. "Not now that it's fixed. 'The Scream' wouldn't let her."

("The Scream" being Jane's respectful pet name for Miss Yelland.)

Dimsie, meanwhile, was scouring the place for the games-captain, and at last, after consulting the practising board, she found her seated at the piano in the lower music-room. Nita looked round in surprise as the excited junior burst into the room after a perfunctory knock.

"What's the matter with you?" she asked coolly. "I really can't be disturbed by you kids in the middle of my practising. Why can't you wait till afterwards?"

"I thought you would like to know as soon as possible," answered Dimsie, "because I've come to tell you that I'm not going to play in the junior match, so there's absolutely no point putting up my name instead of poor Rosamund's."

Nita regarded her in silence for a moment, with a curious sharp glitter in her little black eyes. Then she said calmly:

"I really don't know what things are coming to when kids like you take it upon yourselves to say whether you'll play in a match or not after your name has been put down on the list! But

I warn you, I won't put up with it."

"And I tell you I shan't play," retorted Dimsie stubbornly.

Nita, however, had no intention of being defied by a junior in the Lower Fourth, and her temper, never properly under control, suddenly blazed up.

"Now, just you listen to me, Dimsie Maitland," she commanded hotly. "You will play in the junior match in any case, because, if you go on behaving like this, I shall simply report you to Miss Yelland, and she'll *make* you. I don't suppose you'll be a bit of use to the team, but I intend to make you play – and that's all there is to it! So run away, and don't bother me any more!"

She dashed into loud-pealing arpeggios, as though determined to drown any further argument, and Dimsie, after glancing at her for a moment in speechless fury, rushed off again.

"I told you she'd make you," was Rosamund's dejected comment, when her avenger returned to the tool shed. "Miss Yelland couldn't very well help backing her up. But oh dear! – I did so want to play in that match," and her lips quivered afresh.

"Now, Ros, don't start howling again!" said Dimsie fiercely. "How often have we all told you it doesn't help in the least? Besides, you *shall* play. I don't quite know how I'm to manage it right now, but just leave it to me, and I'll think of a way."

Rosamund and Jean both looked relieved, and even Erica listened to the announcement respectfully, for Dimsie was noted among her companions for "thinking of a way" when difficulties arose.

"Though, all the same," Mabs whispered to Pamela, "she's got her work cut out for her this time!"

Rosamund's misfortune did not go unnoticed by the Upper School, and Nita met with a good deal of criticism among her own circle. With one accord they were all against her, even the faithful Meg.

"Sure, I don't know what you're doing it for, at all," declared the latter. "Even if the child were bad – which she isn't – she can put up a better show than Dimsie Maitland."

"Well, she isn't going to get the chance this time," returned Nita obstinately, with a toss of her head.

Meg shrugged her shoulders and walked away. She was feeling depressed and uncomfortable. The latest news about Primrose was not good; Matron reported a bad night – high temperature and low spirits – neither had the patient's gloom yielded when a batch of notes reached her from her schoolfellows, though they had all tried to write as amusingly as possible. Meg had, of course, been among the correspondents, but she was miserably aware that her letter, despite all efforts, had been constrained and self-conscious. A year ago she would have written to her friend in an easy, natural fashion, full of affectionate teasing and the little school jokes which they had shared together, but now – Meg at last came face to face with the change which had been troubling Primrose for so long. There was a barrier between them, and, try as she would, Meg could not get past it; moreover, she began to realize that the barrier was Nita Tomlinson.

"Suppose Primrose were to get dreadfully ill and die?" she thought, her Celtic imaginationn picturing the direst possibility. "Matron and Miss Yorke both looked awfully grave when they were talking in the passage this afternoon. Faith! I'd never get a chance of making it up with her. They won't let me near her, for fear of the infection, and it's hard to make up by letter when you haven't quarrelled."

It was with some vague idea of making amends that she tried to put in a word for Primrose's little sister, but Nita was quite sharp enough to guess her motive, and this only served to harden her heart yet further against the unlucky Rosamund.

Nita was not at all sorry about this illness of Primrose Garth's. In spite of having gained a very strong influence over Meg, she knew that Primrose was still her rival, and, moreover, she had no illusions about how Meg thought of her. If Primrose had been as good at tennis as she was at cricket, Nita knew that she could never have come between the friends, because in that case it was Primrose who would have been Meg's chosen partner. It seemed fortunate to Nita that her rival should have fallen ill just before the important matches came up, for there was no chance now of those brilliant scores which would have roused the admiration of a girl like Meg, and probably won her back to her former allegiance by making her proud of her friend.

But Nita's feelings were not unmixed. She was sporting enough herself to regret the loss of such a bat for Jane's, and freely admitted that Tony Semple was no substitute. At times she even found herself wishing that Primrose had held out, at least until they had played Westover High School.

"We shan't be so badly off for the others," she thought, "for, by then, Sylvia will be playing again. Well, I've obviously got to make a century against Westover, and if I do – well, I shan't have much fear of losing that idiot Meg then!"

# CHAPTER 17

# JANE'S v. WESTOVER HIGH SCHOOL

The day following was Wednesday, the half-holiday which had been fixed upon for the cricket match with Westover High School, and directly after the midday dinner the visitors arrived. Nita and her team met them and took them down to the playing field, round which the rest of the school had assembled to cheer and criticize. A few Westover girls had come over by the bus or on bicycles to encourage their side, and Dimsie Maitland took charge of some juniors about her own size.

"I see you've brought a strong team," she observed politely to one of the guests. "I remember that tall, fair girl last year – and the freckled one, too – they were awfully good at hockey."

"They're better still at cricket," replied the visitor complacently. "I hear your best bat's in hospital, and Sylvia Drummond has done her foot in. Bad luck for Jane's!"

"Yes, isn't it? But Sylvia can still hit, though she can't run," returned Dimsie hastily, for she detected signs of cockiness in her new friend which she felt it would be well to squash; "and she's got one of us – Pamela Hughes – to run for her, so, really, she's almost better off than if she hadn't sprained her ankle. Pam can run like Jehu."

"Who's Jehu?" inquired the Westuffian.

Dimsie regarded her with pained surprise.

"Don't you do scripture at the High School?" she asked gently.

The visitor flushed with resentment.

"Of course we do," she said, "but not things like that, if that's scripture. We do Joseph, and Samuel, and St Paul's journeys – I don't care for that; one might as well do geography."

"Oh, we did it last term," said Dimsie loftily. "It wasn't bad when Miss Yelland let us keep our maps open. Just now we're doing sort of general knowledge – what people are noted for, and all that. Jehu was a person who was noted for being in a hurry."

"Oh!" rejoined the Westover girl, evidently impressed by the biblical instruction at Jane's. "Look! Our side's going in to bat. They've won the toss."

"I don't mean to be rude," said Dimsie earnestly, "but I hope that's all they do win. No offence meant, you know."

"That's all right," responded the guest, not to be outdone in civility. "I should feel just the same myself. Besides, I can't help being sorry for you; it's really bad luck about the girl with flu – she was such a tremendous bat."

They sat cross-legged on the grass at the extreme edge of the field, and followed every detail of the play with eager attention, though Dimsie's spirits sank as she saw that the Westuffians were giving a very good account of themselves. Not even Vera Robinson, Jane's best bowler, could get near their captain's wicket, no matter how she tried. Three of the enemy retired with nice little scores to their credit, but still the captain held on.

"She's really quite a good player," observed Dimsie with a condescension which veiled her growing anxiety.

"She's not bad," assented her supporter, wrestling with the pride which it would have been improper to show. "She knocked the Eveswood bowling about a bit last week."

"Did – did you beat Eveswood?" queried Dimsie nervously.

"Naturally!" was the lofty response. "In fact, we had to declare in the end. Eveswood isn't putting up much of a show this summer; several of their best girls left at Easter. I should think" (kindly) "your lot might lick them."

"Oh, easily!" returned Dimsie. "We don't play them for a fortnight, and Primrose Garth should be well by then – Hey! Did you see that? Oh, well caught! Brilliant catch, Daph!"

For Daphne Maitland, at cover point, had intercepted a

low ball on its way to the boundary, and the Westover captain was out. Friends and foes alike applauded her vigorously as she walked off to the pavilion, where the board displayed her eighty-three runs.

"Tough luck not to get her century," said Dimsie's companion in disappointed tones. "I always think she's going to, but she never does, quite. Who was the girl with the black ponytail who caught her out?"

"My cousin, Daphne Maitland," replied Dimsie in an offhand voice, as though to convince the stranger that such a performance was an everyday matter at Jane's. "She's fair to middling as a field, but you'll find her a better bat."

"Oh! Then are you the little Maitland girl?" queried the other, regarding her with sudden interest. "That's all right, then. I was told to look out for you."

"I'm not particularly little," retorted Dimsie, with a touch of offence. "I'm in the Lower Fourth this term, and I believe I'm taller than you."

"Oh, I didn't call you that; it was Mother. She used to know your family terribly well when we lived in Scotland, and she only heard recently that you were at the Jane Willard. She gave me a note for your headmistress, asking if you might come to tea with me on Saturday and bring a friend. Do you think you'll be allowed to?"

Dimsie's brown eyes sparkled gleefully.

"Oh, yes; thanks awfully! I haven't been out this term, so I'm sure Miss Yorke will let me. There she is – sitting up by the pavilion with that pink person who brought your team. Let's go and give her the note at once."

The Westuffian (whose name proved to be Dolly Hart) consented readily, and Dimsie led the way, explaining that, if she might really bring a friend, it must be Rosamund Garth, because she'd been having rather a miserable time lately, and this would cheer her up a lot.

They made their way to Miss Yorke and presented Dolly's note, which the headmistress glanced through quickly during the pause between overs. She knew Mrs Hart, and consented at once to her request, and also to Dimsie's plea for Rosamund.

"It is very kind of your mother, dear," she said to Dolly,

"and I am sure they will enjoy themselves very much. Will you ask her from me to return them safely not later than six-thirty? Hullo! Another wicket fallen! Did Hilda Heathley take that?"

Dimsie routed out Rosamund so that she might introduce her to their future hostess, and the three found a new corner from which to view the fray; but the Westover "tail" were not as careful of their wickets as the first five bats, and by tea time they were all out for 128, of which their captain's was by far the largest contribution.

"It's a hideous score to beat," groaned Rosamund, as she and Dimsie plied their guest with buns and very weak tea obtained from the urn in the pavilion, over which Miss Yelland was presiding. "I can hardly eat for thinking of it."

"That's silly!" returned Dimsie, taking a large bite out of her doughnut. "Try one of these, Dolly. Our form made them at the cookery class yesterday, so I know they're good."

"Well, we'd better not eat too much," said Rosamund, "I mean Dimsie and me – 'cause we need to be fit for cheering, and Jane's will need a lot of cheering presently to buck them up."

"I can always cheer, whatever I eat," declared Dimsie. "I never see what difference it makes. After all, it's your throat you cheer with, not . . ."

"Shh!" interrupted Rosamund, with a reproving glare. "Oh look – they're going out already! How quick they've been! Meg's batting first, with Sylvia at the other end. I say, I *am* glad I'm not Pam Hughes! Her knees must be knocking together by now."

"Oh, Pam's all right!" returned Dimsie indifferently. "She's not nervous. I reckon that's why Sylvia chose her. There goes the first ball! Oh, it's dribbling down! I do hope Meg will be careful how she hits."

It was not long, however, before Jane's realized that Meg was not up to her usual form that afternoon. She looked anxious and worried, and her strokes had a touch of uncertainty which alarmed Nita. In fact, at one stage she sent an obvious catch, which the Westover "point" fortunately dropped, and her school-fellows breathed more freely when Sylvia Drummond faced the bowling.

Sylvia was a hard hitter, and Pamela was determined that

the headgirl should not be dismissed through any fault of hers, so between them their score stood at sixteen (including two boundaries) when Meg found herself confronted by the West-over fast bowler. Two minutes later she left the field, stumped, with only ten runs to her credit.

"One wicket for twenty-six! That's jolly good," said Dolly Hart kindly; but Dimsie and Rosamund looked grave. They knew that Nita had been depending on Meg for something better, and the captain of Jane's had a scowl on her face as she went out to take her friend's place.

"What possessed you to let us down like that?" she muttered angrily as she passed Meg.

"Sure, I don't know, unless it's the heat," returned the culprit contritely. "I'm off my stroke entirely today."

Temper is apt to make one's play unreliable, and Nita, swiping out wildly, sent her second ball straight into the hands of "point", who held it this time with determination to redeem her character. Jane's captain walked off again without breaking her duck, and Nancy Harriman took her place.

"Twenty-six for two wickets!" sighed Rosamund. "I do hope Pam will be careful now."

Pam was careful, but not all her efforts could prevent Nancy from running her out, which the agitated senior proceeded to do in a very few minutes. Thirty runs for three wickets, and they had 128 to beat!

Needless to say, they failed to do it, and thereby lost the match, though the remainder of the team, playing with the energy of despair, raised the total to 109 before stumps were drawn at six o'clock. Phyllis Heathley, who was in the eleven solely on account of her fielding, provided a surprise by knocking up forty runs before her bails flew, but hers was the only performance which could, by comparison, be termed brilliant.

"Meg demoralized the lot of us," declared Nita angrily, when they had cheered the victors off the premises. "I never saw such a miserable collapse!"

"Oh, come on, Nita! You were much worse yourself," objected the tactless Nancy. "After all, Meg did break her duck – and you're captain."

"I tell you it was Meg's stupidity that upset me," stormed

Nita. "I can only hope Sylvia's foot will be all right when we play the return on their ground."

"My foot did well enough, thanks to Pam," said Sylvia drily. "The real loss was poor old Primrose. She and Meg are used to going in together and knocking up a few dozen runs between them."

"Well, it just shows how ridiculous it is to depend on a combination like that," said Nita bad-temperedly as she turned away.

# CHAPTER 18

# DIMSIE AND ROSAMUND ABROAD

"Please, Miss Yorke," said Dimsie, tapping at the head-mistress's door next Saturday afternoon, "Rosamund and I are going now."

Miss Yorke looked up from her correspondence.

"Oh, yes! To Mrs Hart's. I had forgotten for the moment. But wait a minute, Dimsie – who is taking you there?"

"Mademoiselle said she'd take us, Miss Yorke. She is going into Westover on her bicycle, but she says she'll walk through St Elstrith and leave us at Mrs Hart's gate."

"But there is no need to take Mademoiselle out of her way," said Miss Yorke quickly. "Two of the seniors are going to tea with Miss Austin, whose house is just a hundred yards further on from the Harts' place. Find Meg Flynn, and tell her I wish you to go with her and Nita."

"Oh, but, please, Miss Yorke," broke in Rosamund, much disturbed by such an arrangement, "Meg and Nita are gone! I saw them setting out just after dinner."

Miss Yorke frowned slightly.

"Are you sure, Rosamund? They haven't reported to me, and I hardly think they would go without doing so."

"They reported to Miss Edgar. I heard Nita say that she couldn't find you."

"Then she can't have looked very far," rejoined the head-mistress drily. "I haven't left this room since dinner time. Well, at any rate, they can bring you back. Go round to Miss Austin's house at a quarter to six, Dimsie, and tell Meg that I wish you to come home in her charge. Now run along, both of you, and have a good time; but don't be late."

"No, Miss Yorke. Thank you. Goodbye," they chorussed, and ran downstairs to join Mademoiselle, who was patiently awaiting them in the hall.

"But I shan't enjoy myself a scrap," moaned Rosamund as they went. "I shall be thinking all the time about the awfulness of having to walk back with Nita."

"Yes, it will be dreadfully awkward," assented Dimsie. "I'm not friends with her myself since she scratched your name off the list of the Lower School eleven."

Nevertheless, they both forgot their school troubles and perplexities in a delightful game of croquet played in the Harts' big, overgrown garden with Dolly and her brothers and sisters. Tea took the form of a picnic in their old summer house, and more games followed till the chimes of the church pealed for half-past five, and Dimsie announced that they must tidy up and go in search of the two seniors.

"Thank you very much for an absolutely super afternoon," she said to Mrs Hart, when bidding her farewell. "Rosamund and I have had a simply smashing time, haven't we, Ros?"

"I must ask Miss Yorke to let you come again before the holidays," said Dolly's mother kindly. "You are sure it's all right about your getting back to school? Because I can easily send some one with you."

"Oh no, thank you," said Dimsie readily. "One of our prefects is having tea with Miss Austin, and we have to call for her there."

"Miss Austin?" echoed Mrs Hart in surprise. "That's odd. She told me this morning, when I met her in the village, that she was spending the afternoon at the tennis club. They're having some open competition, and she's playing in it."

Dimsie looked puzzled.

"Perhaps there's some mistake," she said doubtfully.

"Well, if you find your friends aren't there, come back to me," said Mrs Hart. "I know Miss Yorke wouldn't like you to walk back alone through the country lanes."

Dimsie promised, and she and Rosamund ran off down the road to the little gabled house surrounded by a barberry hedge, which Dolly pointed out to them as being Miss Austin's.

"I hope it's all right," said Rosamund nervously, as her friend pulled the bell.

"If you please," said Dimsie very politely to the young woman who opened it, "are there two big girls here from Jane's?"

"From the Jane Willard Foundation," corrected Rosamund hastily.

"Because they're to take us home," added Dimsie. "Would you say, if they're here, that Rosamund and Dimsie are waiting for them."

The young woman grinned good-humouredly.

"They're not here, love," she answered, "but I can tell you where to find them. They're at the tennis club with Miss Austin. You just go through the village, and it's up a little lane on the right-hand side, where the cottages end. You can't mistake it."

"Thank you very much," responded Dimsie, and led the way down the path again. Outside the barberry hedge once more, she stood still and confronted Rosamund.

"Did you hear that?" she exclaimed. "There's something very peculiar going on! I think those two are playing in this open competition Mrs Hart was talking about."

"Well," said Rosamund placidly, "why shouldn't they? They're our champions."

"But you don't understand!" cried Dimsie, giving her arm a little shake. "Miss Yorke didn't want them to play at that club, 'cause it's gone down and grown rowdy. I heard Daphne and Sylvia talking about it, and they said Nita was furious when Miss Yorke refused the challenge."

Rosamund's blue eyes grew round.

"And you think they've gone and played after all? Oh, crumbs!"

Dimsie caught her hand and tugged her off down the village street. "Come on!" she said determinedly. "Let's go and find out. They've got to take us back to Jane's, and that lady said they were at the tennis club, so we've got to go after them."

They hurried on past the old timbered cottages and quaint little shop windows, which jutted out onto the pavement as though drawing attention to their jumbled wares; boxes and jars filled with sticks of pink and yellow candy jostled sunhats and fishing gear, while yards of bright-coloured streamers festooned pottery souvenirs and picture post-cards. Rosamund was tempted to linger and admire. The juniors from Jane's were not often alone in the village of St Elstrith; but Dimsie drew her on.

"No," she said, "I'm not going to get into a row, and perhaps be stopped going to Dolly's if we're asked there again. As long as we're looking for Meg and Nita, no one can say a word, but we can't expect to find them in shop windows."

Which was so obviously true that Rosamund swallowed her protests and followed meekly on.

At the foot of the little lane leading up to the tennis courts the children halted, for coming down towards them was a group of girls carrying rackets, with a sprinkling of young men among them, their arms about the girls' waists. They were laughing and chattering together in high-pitched voices, with many little squeals and giggles, while right in the midst of them, flushed and excited-looking, walked Meg and Nita.

"There they are!" said Dimsie, wrinkling her small nose fastidiously. "What a horrid crowd!"

At the same moment Nita caught sight of the two juniors, and gave a start of annoyance and dismay.

"Look, Meg!" she exclaimed. "What are those kids doing here? They've no business to be knocking about St Elstrith by themselves. Let's say goodbye, and go and see about it."

At the corner of the lane they extricated themselves from their lively companions with a good deal of laughter and noisy protest, after which Nita literally pounced upon Dimsie and Rosamund, demanding angrily:

"Why are you two hanging round here on your own? A right hole you'll be in, if Miss Yorke hears about this! I never knew such a set of little wretches as you Lower School kids this term – always getting into mischief of some sort!"

Dimsie, who was hot-tempered at the best of times, felt that the rebuke did not come well from Nita, and blazed up accordingly.

"You needn't talk!" she retorted pointedly. "You'll be in a hole yourself when Miss Yorke finds out that you've been playing at that old club after all! She thinks you and Meg are having tea with Miss Austin."

Nita turned scarlet for a moment, then grew pale, and her eyes wavered unpleasantly. Seizing Dimsie by the shoulder, she half dragged, half pushed her through the gate which opened on the field path leading towards St Elstrith's Bay, while Meg and Rosamund followed close behind.

"What do you mean, you little wretch?" hissed the games-captain through her clenched teeth. "What business is it of yours where I go or what I do? Miss Yorke does not think that Meg and I went to tea with Miss Austin – she knows we were at the club, playing in the competition."

Dimsie twisted her shoulder free and looked coldly up at the speaker.

"No, that can't be right," she said bluntly. "Miss Yorke told us you were at Miss Austin's, and that we were to go there at a quarter to six and say that she wanted you to bring us home, 'cause we've been to tea with Dolly Hart. Why are you in such a rage?"

# CHAPTER 19

# DIMSIE'S BARGAIN

Words failed Nita for a moment, and Meg glanced from the big girl to the little one with a shade of anxiety on her face. Could Dimsie be right? Or was it simply some misunderstanding, such as might easily have arisen through confusion of messages? Surely, at least, Nita would not have told a deliberate lie. But in her heart of hearts Meg felt a certain doubtfulness. Two terms' close association with Nita Tomlinson had shown her that her new friend's mind was not as clearly innocent as Primrose Garth's or Sylvia's; Meg had now and again had glimpses of muddy depths which might quite easily be stirred up.

"Nita," she said sharply, "what does it mean? You told me Miss Yorke had given us permission."

Nita tossed her head, and turned away from the two children.

"So she did; but I'm not going to discuss our affairs before a pair of cheeky kids like these," she answered loftily. "If Miss Yorke really told them they were to call for us at a quarter to six, we'd better hurry up, for it's a quarter past now."

"Run on in front, you two," ordered Meg, looking troubled, and the juniors obeyed willingly; they felt it advisable to get as far as possible from Nita in her present mood.

"Now then," said Meg abruptly, turning to her companion, "what is Dimsie talking about?"

Nita shrugged her shoulders and scowled.

"It's most unfortunate that she and that wretched, snivelling little Rosamund were asked out today of all days, but I suppose I shall have to explain things to you. As a matter of fact, I only asked Miss Yorke for permission to go to tea with Miss

Austin; I didn't mention that the tea was to be at her tennis club and that we were to play in the competition.''

Meg came to a standstill in the middle of the path and stared at her, aghast.

''But – but – that was the whole reason for asking special permission – because she didn't want us to play there!''

''She didn't want the school to play there,'' corrected Nita. ''She can't object to what we do as private individuals when we are out for the afternoon.''

''Oh, can't she?'' returned Meg significantly. ''Faith, you'll find she can fast enough! Besides, if you were so sure about it, why didn't you let her know what we were going to do?''

Nita did not answer, as no suitable reply occurred to her for the moment.

''You knew she'd forbid us right away,'' said Meg bitterly, ''but you were so set on showing off before all those outsiders that you couldn't risk it, so you kept it quiet. That's what you did!''

''I thought they'd imagine we'd refused their challenges because we were afraid to meet them,'' muttered Nita. ''I wanted to show we could beat them easily, and we jolly well did!''

But Meg's pleasure in her triumph had completely faded.

''Of course we did! They were useless – at tennis and everything. I'm not surprised Miss Yorke didn't want Jane's to mix with them. And it's all very well for you, Nita; you'll get into an awful row, but that's something you never care about. What do you suppose will happen to me, seeing I'm a prefect and have been twice as long at the school?''

''Now, listen to me, and don't get so excited,'' argued Nita persuasively. ''Thanks to my care and foresight, you'll get off with nothing but a lecture about taking the permission for granted and trusting too much to me. You ought to be grateful instead of making such a fuss. Why do you suppose I kept it back from you – what Miss Yorke had really given us leave for, I mean?''

''Because you knew I shouldn't go under such circumstances,'' retorted Meg promptly.

Nita looked rather taken aback.

"Oh, well! If you like to think that, of course – but it was really to keep you out of a mess. I didn't mind so much for myself, because I felt it would be worth it – and I still think so."

"Well, I don't!" returned Meg shortly. "I don't consider a few sets of tennis are worth risking the loss of my prefectship."

They crossed the next field in troubled silence, Dimsie and Rosamund keeping well ahead. At last Nita said, with a side-long glance at her companion:

"But why need you lose it? Why should Miss Yorke hear anything about it at all? Those kids may be cheeky and tire-some, but they've been long enough at Jane's to know that sneaking isn't done."

Meg stared at her in surprise.

"Of course they wouldn't sneak, but that isn't the point. The only decent thing for me to do now is to go and tell Miss Yorke . . ." She stopped short at the sight of Nita's expression.

"Precisely!" said that young lady coldly. "Tell Miss Yorke that you're very sorry, but you quite thought we had permission to play this afternoon – that I told you I'd asked for it, and got it, right? What's that, if it's not sneaking, may I ask?"

"You said you didn't mind the row," Meg mumbled.

"I said I shouldn't mind if we were found out, because it would have been worth it, but I do mind your wriggling out of it at my expense! I meant, if it ever came out, to own up that you sinned in ignorance, but that's rather different from being offered up as a sacrifice to your conscience – or your prefect-ship!"

Meg groaned, too depressed to flare up at the sneer.

"Oh, I see that plainly enough! I didn't think for the moment. No, I certainly can't go to Miss Yorke without your permission."

"And that you'll never have," declared Nita, with rising spirits. "It would be perfectly absurd to go and make an un-called-for fuss about it. It isn't likely Miss Yorke will ever run across anyone belonging to the club except Miss Austin, and she's going away for a couple of months on Monday. All we've got to do is to caution those two little idiots not to gossip among the girls, and we shall be as right as rain."

"I don't agree with you," said Meg sullenly. "I hate the whole business, and that's the truth! But I can do nothing if you tie me up like this."

"Well, I do," insisted Nita, and putting her hands to her mouth she called out to the pair in front.

Dimsie and Rosamund paused till the seniors came up with them, when Nita said severely:

"Now, look here, you two! You're not to go chattering to everybody in Jane's about meeting Meg and me coming away from the tennis club. Do you understand? We've got reasons of our own for not wanting the whole school to hear about it, and we shall make things pretty hot for you if we catch you telling tales – see?"

"Pooh!" said Dimsie impudently. "*You* can't do anything to us! And Meg wouldn't."

A nasty look came into Nita's little black eyes.

"Can't I?" she asked. "Didn't I stop Rosamund from playing in that ridiculous match of yours?"

A sudden inspiration flashed across Dimsie's nimble brain.

"You haven't stopped her yet," she replied stoutly; "you've only struck her off the list. I know quite well why you don't want us to tell the others where we met you this evening, so you needn't pretend, Nita Tomlinson, even if you *are* captain of games and all that! I shan't talk about it and neither will Rosamund, on one condition – and that is that you put her straight back in the junior eleven."

A sort of gasp came from Meg and from Rosamund, while Dimsie herself turned cold inside at her own audacity. Only for her friend's sake would she have ventured on such a dangerous act. She shut her eyes tightly and waited for the sky to fall in, but nothing happened, so she opened them again and stared defiantly at Nita.

"What do you mean, you little sneak?" cried the older girl furiously, finding her voice at last.

"I'm not a sneak, and you needn't call me names," retorted Dimsie. "It would be sneaking to tell Miss Yorke or any of the teachers, but if I tell Sylvia or Daphne it's only interfering, and I don't in the least mind interfering if I can get poor old Rosamund back into the eleven by doing it."

For the next five minutes Nita stormed, argued, coaxed, but all to no purpose. Dimsie stood there like a small rock in pink cotton, perfectly aware now that she had the whip hand of the senior and determined to gain the day for Rosamund. Such a chance had befallen her as she had never hoped for in her wildest dreams. She did not enjoy her position, and for any other cause she would have given in almost at once; but she had sworn to redress Rosamund's wrongs, and the battle, it seemed, had been given into her hands.

"Come along," said Meg impatiently at last. "You can't stand here arguing all night with a junior! We're late as it is, and that's got to be explained. What on earth does it matter who plays in the match? You'd better give in to her, Nita, or let me go to Miss Yorke."

It was a bitter pill for Nita to swallow. She turned on her heel and strode off without a word in the direction of the school buildings where they showed above the trees on the crest of the downs. But that evening the juniors were surprised and relieved to see Dimsie's name scratched off the list of the junior eleven and Rosamund's restored.

# CHAPTER 20

# LOST UNDERGROUND

Sunday was a hot day, so hot that some of the girls flagged considerably during the long, shadeless walk back from church across the fields. Dimsie and Pamela Hughes were both thoroughly over-tired and disinclined for their dinner – a symptom which was sufficiently unusual to startle Miss Moffatt, their form-mistress, who at once reported them to Matron in case they'd caught the flu. So far Primrose Garth's had been the only case, but school-mistresses always go in fear of epidemics.

"It's only the heat," said Matron serenely, when she had inspected them. "Don't go out into the garden until after five o'clock. Let me see – your dormitory should be nice and cool just now, with the sun off it. Suppose you go and lie down on your beds until tea time."

Dimsie and Pam assented languidly and went upstairs together slowly to their bedroom. However, an hour's rest proved quite enough to revive them, and they cast about in their minds for a profitable way of spending the remaining hour before the tea gong should ring. They knew from past experience that they must not go downstairs till their sentence had expired; Matron had fixed tea time as the limit, and her commands were as the laws of the Medes and Persians.

"But I wish we'd thought of bringing up our books with us," observed Dimsie regretfully, sitting up in bed with her knees clasped to her chin.

"I'm not exactly in the mood for reading now," returned Pamela. "I feel so much better that I want to do something. I wish we could have an adventure."

"How can we, upstairs in the dormitory? Why, Pam, what

do you mean? Why are you looking so funny?"

"Because I've just had a perfectly mag-*nif*-icent inspiration!" declared Pamela, bouncing excitedly on her bed. "Don't you remember what Mabs Hunter told us on the first night of the term – about that prefect's grandfather and the secret passage?"

"Oh!" said Dimsie, her eyes growing round. "Yes, I remember now, but this term has been so full of things that I never gave it another thought, and I don't believe Mabs has either."

"Oh, she did!" replied Pam. "But she's never had a chance to explore properly. You see, we're always in such a hurry in this dormitory, either getting up or going to bed or changing, that there's no time left over. But listen, Dimsie, now's our chance! Let's feel along the walls thoroughly and press any lumps that might be hidden springs."

"All right, let's!" assented Dimsie. "Though I don't somehow believe it'll be much use, Pam. The walls in this room look so very modern."

"That's because of the wallpaper," said Pamela. "Nobody knows what may be underneath."

This was undeniable, and Dimsie obediently fingered her way along the stretch of wall portioned off to her by her friend, while Pamela herself pushed her arm as far behind the chest of drawers as she could persuade it to reach.

"I've made an awful mess of my best clean dress," she remarked, ruefully regarding her sleeve as she drew it out. "I don't know what Miss Rankin will say when she sees it."

"Never mind," returned Dimsie philosophically, "it's only white embroidery stuff. We can wash it in the basin at bedtime when you take it off, and you won't want it again till next Sunday. But, Pam, it's absolutely pointless pawing along these walls, for I've just come to a place where a nail has torn the paper, and it's all plaster underneath. You can never find secret springs in plaster."

"No," said Pamela reluctantly, "I suppose you can't. What a nuisance, though!"

"And if you take my advice," added Dimsie, "you'll change into an ordinary dress now, and we can spend the rest of the time getting that sleeve clean. It is rather mucky, and the first mistress who sees you going into tea will spot it at once."

"I'm afraid so," agreed Pamela. "Just undo my zip at the back, will you?"

Dimsie complied, and Pamela slipped out of the dirty dress and into the cupboard in search of a clean one. It was a deep cupboard, running back into the wall (as was the case in most of the dormitories at Jane's), and capable of containing the coats and dresses of everyone in the room. Pamela's clothes were hanging on the rail at the very end, and as she seized the hanger to lift out her every-day dress she slipped and her hand struck against the wooden panelling behind with a hollow sound. It was a thing which must have happened countless times before throughout the term, but never before had Pamela noticed the peculiarity; now, with her mind full of the hidden passage for which she had been searching, she called out:

"Hey, Dimsie, come in here for a moment! The walls of this cupboard aren't plastered, anyhow! Listen!"

She pushed aside the hanging dresses and rapped with her knuckles on the wood.

"It does sound funny," admitted Dimsie. "Is it the same all the way up?"

Springing onto the shelf where suitcases were kept, in order to reach higher, Pam all but overbalanced, and clutched at a peg on the cupboard wall to save herself. The peg came away in her hand, and before their astonished eyes a long crack slowly widened from floor to ceiling. She had found the secret lever and the panel was moving back!

Perhaps the works were rusty from long disuse, perhaps the door was never intended to open very wide; whatever the reason, it presently stuck fast, leaving an opening barely wide enough for the girls to squeeze through.

In a moment, when they had recovered their breath, Pam whisked her dress over head and fumbled feverishly with the fastenings.

"Do me up, Dimsie; please do me up quickly! We've got to find out where this leads to without a minute's delay!"

"Okay – quick!" cried Dimsie, tugging ruthlessly at hooks

and eyes. "But wait till I get Erica's torch, for it's quite dark in there."

It did not take long to find the torch, and its unlicensed borrowers remembered with satisfaction that Erica had recently fitted a new battery and had hardly used it since. With adroit wriggles they pushed themselves through the opening and stood in the queer, musty atmosphere of the secret passage.

"Wait a minute – don't move!" cried Pam peremptorily, and switched on the light, adding, "I thought so!" triumphantly, for they stood at the head of a flight of steps leading downwards into the gloom.

"Thank heavens we stood still!" exclaimed Dimsie devoutly. "I was just going forward when you stopped me. Hey, Pam! What an adventure! Where do you suppose this goes to?"

"That's what I'm going to find out," returned Pamela promptly. "Come on, Dimsie! Oh, isn't this the most incredible thing that ever happened?"

Down the stone steps they went, in the thickness of the wall, with the torch throwing its circle of light before them. It seemed as though the stairs would never end, but at length the two explorers reached the bottom and turned sharply to the left along a very narrow passage, where they could only walk in single file. Somewhere through the left-hand wall they could faintly hear people talking and laughing, and Pam, who was leading, paused for a moment to listen.

"Where are they?" she queried. "Where are *we*, if we can hear them so plainly?"

Dimsie knitted her brows in a puzzled fashion.

"I suppose," she said slowly, "we must be in the outside wall of the mistresses' sitting-room. I'm sure that was Mademoiselle's funny, high-up little laugh."

They went on for a few yards further, then Pamela halted again.

"Look!" she said. "Quite a lot of passages all meet together here. Isn't this exciting? Which way shall we go now?"

"I know!" cried Dimsie. "Let's take this one which turns off to the right, because it must go straight under the garden, and perhaps we'll find it comes out in the wood. There was a big rabbit burrow . . ."

"Not big enough for us to get through," interrupted Pam decidedly. "There isn't a burrow in the wood big enough for that; but come on, and we'll see where it goes to. We can explore the others later."

Accordingly they pressed on down the righthand passage, which seemed to go twisting and turning interminably through the depths of the earth, sometimes dipping down a long slope, sometimes climbing up, till at last Dimsie protested breath-lessly:

"Pam, we've walked miles and miles and miles – I don't think we ought to go any further just now. Suppose the tea bell rings and they send up to see what's become of us? It would be awfully difficult to explain."

"Oh, we mustn't explain!" said Pamela, retracing her steps unwillingly. "This must be our deadly secret from every-body but the Anti-Soppists, and, above all, from any sort of mistress. We'd never be allowed to come down here again, and there must be masses to discover if only we had time."

"All right," agreed Dimsie, "we'll only tell our own lot. But I think we ought to start going back now – it must be pretty nearly tea time."

They hurried back along the way by which they had come, breaking every now and then into a little run, for the floor of the passage was fairly hard and even. Both were panting when they arrived at the spot where the various lanes converged, and just at that moment, far away and muffled, came the sound of the big brass gong in the hall.

"There!" exclaimed Dimsie. "Didn't I tell you so? What a good thing we turned back when we did! Up this way, isn't it?"

They darted up the nearest turning and hurried on, ex-pecting every moment to find themselves at the foot of the stone steps, but the passage curved and twisted and proved so much longer than they expected that they began to realize there must be some mistake.

"Crikey, Dimsie, we *shall* be late!" said Pamela anxiously, as they dashed back again. "Fancy going down the wrong turning like that! Let's stop and think which way we came."

They stood at the meeting of the ways and racked their memories for any outstanding feature which had marked their particular passage as different from the rest, but neither of them could recall anything of the sort.

"It might be this one," said Dimsie uncertainly, taking a few steps forward, but Pamela pulled her back.

"Of course not, silly! That's the way we've just come. I think it's the one exactly opposite."

"No, because ours turned sharply off at once. You can see that's straight."

They stood still for a moment in silence; then Dimsie, who was carrying the torch, suddenly shut it off.

"We'd better save the light to use when we're moving about," she remarked calmly, though her voice shook a little, "'cause we might as well face it, Pam. We've gone and got lost!"

# CHAPTER 21

# THE FINDING OF SYLVIA'S NOTE-BOOK

The predicament in which they found themselves was not a pleasant one, and Pamela observed in rather uncertain tones:

"I . . . think I'm a bit scared, aren't you?"

In her heart of hearts Dimsie was, but she did not mean to admit it.

"What's the good of being scared?" she returned stoutly. "We'll soon find the way out. It just means going down the passages, one after another, till we hit on the right one."

"But – how do you know which we've tried already? They all look so much alike."

"Let's do as if it was a maze," suggested Dimsie practically. "If we go down a wrong tunnel, turn back again and try the next on the left. Don't worry Pam, we're bound to hit on the one we want if we keep on trying the left!"

There was so much sound sense in the theory that Pamela, who was basically quite unperturbable, cheered up at once, and hand in hand the pair started off once more. A few yards down their new venture they found a branching passage, along which Dimsie plunged unhesitatingly.

"Now we're all right," she cried. "This is where we heard Mademoiselle talking in the teachers' room. The stairs must be round the next bend."

"It seems rather a long bend," ventured Pam dejectedly, when they had pushed forward for a considerable distance.

"It is," admitted Dimsie. "P'raps we'd better turn again. Oh, but – that's funny!"

"What?"

"Well, I think we're back in the long tunnel we went down

first of all. I remember that queer-shaped stone sticking in the wall."

"Then if we turn back here," said Pam hopefully, "we'll come out where we started from, and if we stand still there and think very carefully, I expect we'll remember which opening to take for the stairs."

"And if not," added Dimsie, "we can go to the left again."

So, having decided this point, they marched forward undauntedly as before.

"I don't remember," remarked Pam presently, "that the stone was quite so far along. Yet we don't seem to be anywhere near the beginning of the tunnel."

"We've been tramping around for hours," declared Dimsie. "Surely, when we get round this corner – oh, Pam!"

They had turned the corner, and stood staring in astonishment, for there, ahead of them, glimmered a round patch of light; and when they stopped talking, they could distinctly hear the beat of the waves as they broke against the high chalk cliffs.

"I know what's happened!" cried Pamela. "We've got so muddled with twisting and turning that this time we've been walking away from the house as hard as we could, and we're coming into one of those caves that we've so often seen up on the cliff face when we've been paddling at low tide."

"That's all right, then!" exclaimed Dimsie triumphantly. "It's one way home, even if it isn't the shortest."

"Well, it's shorter than playing blind man's buff in a rabbit burrow," retorted Pam, "especially as I've thought for some time that the torch was growing dimmer."

"So have I," confessed Dimsie, "but I didn't say anything, 'cause I hoped you hadn't noticed it. The battery's going."

It did not take them long to cover the few yards between them and daylight, but the expiring torch flickered out as they stumbled past an old broken crate and into a small, low-roofed cave, cheerful with the sunshine which streamed through its seaward opening. The two girls leaned eagerly out, and then drew back to gaze at each other in silent dismay, for their cave was situated nearly two hundred feet up the face of the cliff, below which an almost full tide was dashing on the weed-covered rocks.

"And that's your nice, short way home!" moaned Pamela bitterly.

"It was you who said it was short – I didn't!" snapped Dimsie.

"Well, you said it *was* the way home, anyhow," contended Pam, "and unless you're expecting a helicopter to fetch us, we're no better off than before."

"How was I to know, stupid? The other caves are quite near the shore. Anyhow, it won't help us to squabble. We've got to stay here till somebody finds us, because we'll only come to a much worse end if we try to go back along those passages without a light."

Pamela's jaw dropped, and for one perilous moment her eyes filled with tears.

"But – but, Dimsie, we'll starve! How can anyone ever find us here when they haven't the faintest idea where to look? And it's past tea time – and I'm hungry already . . ."

Dimsie seized her fiercely by the shoulders and gave her a little shake.

"You needn't call yourself an Anti-Soppist if you're going to behave like that, for you're being about as soppy now as it's possible to be! Look, anyone passing in a boat will see us directly if we shout and wave to them, so sit on that stone there, close to the hole, and keep a look out. I'm surprised at you, Pam Hughes! You said you wanted an adventure, and now that you've got one you're practically crying about it!"

"I'm not!" denied Pamela hotly.

"Well, don't then! Just watch for a boat while I explore the cave. I expect smugglers must have used it once, and carried their bales and casks along those secret tunnels to Jane Willard's house. P'raps her family were smugglers."

Pamela was interested, but raised an objection nevertheless.

"How could they get their stuff up here in the first place?" she asked.

"Dragged it up with ropes from the shore below?" suggested Dimsie. "But that must have given them an awful lot of bother, for this place is almost at the top of the cliff. Look at that queer crack in the roof, Pam! The light comes through, so it must open out in the grass there."

"There is a crack near the wall of the old lighthouse grounds," returned Pamela, without any great show of interest. "I've often dropped pebbles through, and wondered where they went to. Anyhow, it isn't wide enough for us to get out by."

"We couldn't reach up to it if it was," replied Dimsie promptly, and continued her voyage of discovery into the dark recesses of their cavern. "I say, Pam!" she exclaimed presently from behind a rock which jutted out in one corner, "I've found out how the smugglers got their bales up."

"What to do you mean?" inquired Pamela, deserting her post to follow the explorer; and she uttered a cry of astonishment when she found behind the big boulder a flight of steps cut out of the stone and going down a dark funnel which, apparently, pierced its way into another much lower cave. Her spirits rose at once, for Pamela was not without daring.

"Let's go down!" she cried. "It may take us right to the shore, and when the tide turns . . ."

"We shall do nothing of the sort," interrupted Dimsie with decision, "so there! Not while we can hope for a boat to pass and rescue us."

"But how can the boat rescue us, if it does pass?" Pam argued. "They can't reach us."

"They can tell the coastguard at St Elstrith, and they'll bring ropes and pull us up from the top, or something like that; but I'm not going down those steps without a light – not unless we're dying of starvation. If the torch hadn't run out it would have been different."

"That's a rotten torch! And I shall tell Erica so, when I see her," declared Pam disgustedly. "Either that, or the battery was a dud."

Dimsie had gone back into the centre of the cave again, and with an exclamation of surprise she picked up something small and thick and square against which her foot had knocked.

"Well!" she said. "That's the most extr'ordinary and mysterious thing that's ever happened! Here's Sylvia's lost note-book – the one with all our characters in it, you know, that Nita Tomlinson said Rosamund had taken."

"I don't believe it!" cried Pamela, staring at it round-eyed with curioisity. "It's almost like magic! However do you think it came here?"

Dimsie shook her brown curls in perplexity.

"It must be magic," she declared, and her tone was awed as she added, "or else do you think it could possibly be a miracle, Pam? You see, I'd promised Rosamund to find it somehow, because of it being so badly on her mind, and I've put it in my prayers every night since."

"Of course it's a miracle," said Pamela decidedly, "and it has cheered me up a good deal, Dimsie, because, you know, now we've found the note-book, somebody will be sure to find us; otherwise it would be such a waste of the miracle, and it wouldn't be a bit of good to Rosamund."

"Yes, it would be quite wasted," assented Dimsie, greatly struck by this line of argument. "Besides, that's put an idea into my head." She paused, reddened, and kicked away a pebble with her foot. "I don't know what you think about it, Pam, but it seems to me it might help things on a little if we prayed for a boat or something of that sort."

"Do you mean out loud?" asked Pam shyly.

"Not unless you'd rather. I didn't mean a proper prayer meeting, you know, but just quietly in to ourselves. Only we'd beter do it both at the same time, don't you think?"

So, clasping hands, the two girls knelt on the rough floor of the cave and prayed "in to themselves" for deliverance from this strange prison into which they had strayed, while outside the gulls went fishing among the floating seaweed and the little waves dashed themselves against the high cliffs in noisy play.

# CHAPTER 22

# NITA MAKES A SUGGESTION

Nita Tomlinson, meanwhile, was spending the Sunday afternoon in thinking out fresh schemes for getting the better of her adversaries, among whom she now condescended to include Dimsie Maitland. Indeed, on turning the matter over in her mind, she came to the conclusion that her score against Dimsie was a fairly heavy one. Not only had this intrepid junior "cheeked" her beyond all belief and forced her hand in the affair of Rosamund, but she had at the same time exposed the shady side of Nita's character to Meg Flynn in a fashion which had been, to say the least of it, extremely awkward.

At this point in her musings Nita's black brows came together in a thunderous scowl. Her instinct warned her that she had lost ground with Meg which it would be hard to regain, if she ever succeeded in doing so at all. This meant a triumph for Primrose as soon as she came out of hospital to enjoy it. Altogether Nita decided that Dimsie had prepared a bitter cup of humiliation for her, and must be repaid accordingly; yet it was rather a nuisance, for, in spite of all that had come and gone, Nita had a sneaking liking for this small enemy of hers.

Armed with a book, the games-captain sought out a shady corner of the garden, but she did not read. Her whole mind was bent for the time being on crushing the little worm who had dared to turn against her superiors, and Nita's mind was fairly acute; it did not take long to arrive at a very neat scheme, which would not only defeat Dimsie, but put an end to this ridiculous match in which Sylvia and Primrose had interested themselves so much.

Nita's black eyes gleamed with pleasure as she worked out

the plan which she could only regard in the light of an inspiration. At length she closed her book with a bang, and went in search of Miss Yelland. The sports-mistress, however, was not to be found, having gone to tea with a friend at Eastcliff.

"All the better," decided Nita. "I can now go straight to headquarters. If Miss Yorke will let me put up a notice at once, nobody else can raise any objections – and she's less likely to remember that junior match than Miss Yelland, who's been down to see the kids practise."

Miss Yorke had also gone into the garden with a book to while away the hour before tea, but the book was interesting and she was really reading it, so it was with some difficulty that she suppressed a grunt of impatience when, between the low boughs of the cedar tree, she saw Nita bearing down upon her. A headmistress is supposed to regard her pupils without preference, but Miss Yorke was human, and though she did her best and was almost unduly severe to the girls for whom she had a sneaking fondness, she could not altogether hide her distaste for Nita Tomlinson, whose devious ways had more than once roused her contempt. In duty bound, Miss Yorke had tried to instil something of the standards of Jane's into its games-captain, but so far her efforts had been unavailing, and she felt an uneasy dread that such a girl as Nita might in time lower the tone of the school.

"Well, my dear, what can I do for you?" she asked, laying down her book as the girl came up to her.

Nita seated herself on the ground, there being no second chair available, and said:

"I have an idea about which I'd like to ask you, Miss Yorke. You know how many of us have been going down regularly to the bay this term for swimming lessons – all the Upper School, and a good many of the younger ones too. Wouldn't it be possible to get up some sort of water sports there on half-term Saturday?"

Miss Yorke looked interested.

"That's a good idea, Nita. You're all so keen on tennis and cricket that I sometimes feel you don't take full advantage of being at school so near the sea; and, of course, at this time of the summer, before the visitors arrive, you have the bay practically to yourselves. Have you talked it over with Miss Yelland?"

"Not yet," Nita answered. "I only thought of it myself this afternoon; and she is out, so I thought I'd consult you about it. We haven't many days before half-term now, you see, and so the sooner it's fixed up the better."

"That's true," assented Miss Yorke. "What do you propose to have in the way of events?"

"Ordinary open races, dormitory races, diving," replied Nita promptly, "tub races, apple hunts . . ."

"What's that?" interposed Miss Yorke.

"Someone will row out to the raft, taking a basket of apples with them; then the competitors will dive off from the rocks and swim across to the raft. While they do so, the apples will be emptied into the sea – one for each swimmer, who has to catch it in her mouth and bring it to shore."

Miss Yorke laughed.

"Like a dog with a stick! It sounds quite a good notion. Yes, certainly, Nita, I have no objection to your arranging a water fête, provided you engage old Tom and his boat to stay near you all the time in case of accidents. Better see Miss Yelland about the arrangements when she comes back tonight. As you say, there isn't much time to lose."

Nita rose to her feet, brushing cedar needles off the yellow pleats of her Sunday dress.

"Then we may fix it for half-term Saturday?" she persisted.

Miss Yorke's thoughts were turning back with longing to the book on her lap. She got so little time for reading, and there was still half an hour before tea.

"Yes, of course," she said absently, "it's quite a convenient day."

"That's what I thought," said Nita smoothly; "and, Miss Yorke, it would save time, wouldn't it, if I stuck up the official notice on the board, just to let the girls know about it? Miss Yelland can settle the details afterwards."

"Oh, yes, if you like," responded Miss Yorke. "At least, if you are sure there's nothing else down on the fixture card for that date? I know our Saturdays are pretty well filled up."

"I am quite sure," replied Nita, with a curious smile

lurking at the corners of her mouth. After which she departed, and Sabbath peace brooded once more about the headmistress of Jane's.

Five minutes later, Hilda Heathley, taking a letter to the post-box in the hall, saw the games-captain retreating and a new notice – headed: "Attention! Water Fête!" in big red letters – fastened to the board.

"Great idea!" she remarked approvingly, as she read it. "I must go and tell the others. We've never had anything like that before, and it ought to be super fun."

The Sixth Form, for the most part, were lolling about the senior sitting-room, having decided that it was too hot out of doors. They received Hilda's news with acclamation, and one or two went in search of Nita to hear more about it. Only Sylvia, resting her nearly-recovered foot on a stool, exclaimed suddenly:

"Half-term Saturday? Is that official, Hilda?"

"Yes; it's got 'By order of Miss Yorke' below Nita's signature."

"But it can't be – that's the day of the juniors' match! What can Nita be thinking of?"

"How she can best put a spoke in your wheel, I should imagine," returned Joyce Lamond grimly. "Remember, that date hasn't been booked for the match, Sylvia. The list of the team has been posted, but not the date."

Sylvia frowned with frustration and drummed impatient fingers on the arm of her chair. It was one of the unwritten laws of fair play at Jane's, with regard to sporting fixtures of any sort, that time and place belonged to the team who first got their official notice pinned up on the board in the hall; any notice which had been approved by Miss Yorke was, of course, official.

"It's sickening!" exclaimed Daphne Maitland indignantly. "Those kids have been practising like little Trojans, and this will absolutely squash their match! The Middle School made a favour of playing them at all, and now they'll simply throw it up at once – they're crazy about swimming."

"Very unsporting of them if they do." commented Hilda. "And yet – you can understand the water fête being an irresistible temptation. Couldn't the match be played on Monday?

After all, that's a whole holiday too."

"No, it couldn't," said Sylvia shortly. "Jean and Erica are both going home from Saturday night till Tuesday morning – Winnie Hatton too. I suppose we might hold the Middle School to it, but they'd be unwilling, to say the least of it, probably sulky."

"Besides," added Daphne disgustedly, "the whole thing would fall flat. Every single soul except the players would be down in the bay. Poor kids! And poor Primrose, who spent so much time and trouble coaching them!"

"You may be sure friend Nita took *that* into consideration," observed Joyce.

Sylvia pulled herself up out of her chair as the tea gong sounded.

"I refuse to be beaten by a trick like this," she declared resolutely. "I shall get the school together and put it to the vote, that's what!"

Hilda Heathley shook her head doubtfully as they moved towards the dining-room door.

"They'll vote for the thing that will interest them most," she declared. "That's only human nature."

"Well, then, they've jolly well got to be inhuman for once!" growled Sylvia.

# CHAPTER 23

# RESCUED

Afternoon tea at Jane's was a casual meal, when everybody sat round the tables in the big dining-room in whatever order they liked. Only the mistress in charge was bound to be present, though occasionally another would stroll in from the more select meal in the teachers' room. Consequently Dimsie and Pamela were not missed at first, until Miss Moffatt filled the last cup at the big urn and had time to look about her.

"Two short at the junior table!" she exclaimed. "Oh, of course! Matron told me Pam and Dimsie were lying down. Run up and tell them, Jean. They can't have heard the gong."

Jean obediently ran, but came back in a few minutes with the news that the dormitory was empty.

"Nonsense!" exclaimed Miss Moffatt. "They must be hiding somewhere, naughty little girls! One of the seniors might . . . Phyllis, just go up and bring them down, dear. Their tea will be perfectly cold."

Phyllis Heathley went off in her turn, and stayed a little longer, but she, too, came back with the same tale – Pam and Dimsie were nowhere to be seen.

"And a nice mess they've left your dormitory in!" she added, in passing, to Erica Innes. "Beds crumpled, clothes on the floor, cupboard door open; if you're monitress, you'd better see about it after tea."

Erica glowered indignantly.

"Wait till I see them," she muttered, as the big girl passed on. "If Dimsie and Pam have gone on the spree, they might have had the decency to leave the place tidy. I shan't clear up after them just because I'm monitress. They can jolly well come back and do it themselves!"

Miss Moffatt, meanwhile, decided that the truants were up to pranks of some sort, and that it would be undignified to pursue them further. When they were hungry they would probably appear; they knew when tea would be cleared away and their chance of a meal gone.

When the last party of stragglers had left the dining-room, however, and there was still no sign of the missing pair, the mistress became uneasy, and was on her way upstairs to investigate when she met Erica flying down in search of her.

"Oh, Miss Moffatt, do come!" she began breathlessly. "I thought p'raps I'd better go and put our room straight, after all, and there's a peg pulled out in the cupboard – and a crack down the back of it – and I think they must have found that secret passage of Mabs Hunter's, and gone down it."

"What *are* you talking about?" demanded Miss Moffatt. "If Mabs knows where the secret passage is, it's more than anybody else does."

"Oh, she didn't know – she only guessed – but I do believe they've found it. Please come, Miss Moffatt!"

Through the mysterious means whereby news flies all around a big school in no time, Jane's quickly became aware of what had happened, and volunteer search parties arrived from all directions on the upper landing, where the headmistress herself had by this time taken command.

"I don't know," said Miss Yorke coldly, "why the whole school is running about the passages this afternoon. Will you all kindly go back to where you came from, and send the prefects here?"

The would-be searchers melted hastily away. Supervision was always lax on Sundays, and they felt it would be a pity if it were tightened owing to any ill-judged act of theirs. The prefects arrived in due course, and followed Miss Yorke and the matron into the dormitory, where Erica was eagerly displaying her discovery.

"Yes," said Miss Yorke, using enough force to push the panel back a little further. "It certainly is the lost stairway. The vicar was talking about it to me lately," she added to Miss Rankin. "He says that old Squire Willard – Jane's father – was known to be in league with the smugglers, and there is a long tunnel leading to some cave in the cliffs which they were in the habit of using. Where Dimsie and Pamela Hughes have got to I can't think, but according to the vicar, there are various passages leading to different emergency exits in the grounds which the smugglers could use in case of discovery, and probably those unfortunate children have lost themselves in the rabbit warren."

Miss Rankin gave vent to a sceptical sniff.

"Probably they're not unfortunate at all," she commented. "Knowing that pair, it wouldn't surprise me to find them having the time of their lives down there, without giving a thought to other people's anxiety."

Miss Yorke shook her head and smiled. She knew her girls – even the little ones – well.

"They're not that sort," she said confidently, "not Pam and Dimsie. Come along, girls! We shall have to divide into four search parties of two each presently, when we come to the branching passages. Yes, Erica – I am counting you in – you deserve it, for you found the open panel. You can come with me."

One or two of the girls ran back for torches, and Miss Yorke armed herself with a large old-fashioned lantern, after which they squeezed themselves one by one through the narrow opening and filed down the steep stone steps.

"What an adventure!" murmured Meg to Joyce Lamond. "Faith! I wouldn't have missed this for the world!"

"Wait till we can come down and do a little exploring on our own," returned Joyce gaily. "Fancy living on the top of all this for years and never knowing it!"

"I should be more interested if I knew that the kids were safe," said Daphne Maitland from behind. "These subterranean passages have been known to fall in at times – no, no, silly! not these particular ones," in reply to a startled exclamation from Meg, "but, of course, they just might."

"Don't talk rhubarb!" replied Joyce bluntly. "You're worried about that cheeky little cousin of yours, and I don't blame you."

They had reached the wider space where the other passages branched off, and here Miss Yorke paused to give further directions.

"Sylvia, you and Daphne can try that opening there, while Joyce and Meg take the next. You and Daisy might try the one opposite, Miss Rankin, and I shall take Erica down here with me. I've no idea how long these tunnels are, but go as far as you can and call their names as you go. When you turn back, wait here till we all arrive."

She drew out her handkerchief and laid it at the mouth of the passage down which they had just come.

"Safer to blaze our homeward trail," she observed lightly. "It wouldn't do for us all to be lost in the depths!"

The searchers parted on their different routes, and muffled calls reached their ears from time to time as other parties shouted to Dimsie and Pam in accordance with Miss Yorke's directions. It was all very eerie and strange, and the rescuers felt a good deal of pity for the two juniors who had contrived to lose themselves in such a creepy maze.

"The air is growing fresher, Erica," declared Miss Yorke suddenly, when she and her small companion had walked for a few minutes in silence.

Erica wrinkled up her nose questingly, rather like a dog on an interesting scent.

"There's a sort of seaweedy smell," she remarked. "Can you smell it, Miss Yorke?"

"I believe I do; anyhow, the mustiness is less. Shout again, dear. They may be round that corner."

Erica put her hands to her mouth and shouted with a yodelling cry peculiar to the members of the Anti-Soppist Society. For the first time there seemed to be a faint response from the distance ahead. Erica broke into a run, and Miss Yorke followed with a fleetness which at any other time would have struck the junior as strange in anyone so venerable as a headmistress must naturally be. Just then, however, they caught a glimpse of daylight in the distance, and a distinct shout echoed down the passage.

"Oh, help! Help, whoever it is! We're lost!"

"All right, my dears, we're coming!" called Miss Yorke in ringing tones, and in another minute she was on her knees in the cave with an arm round each of her lost lambs.

"You poor little girls! What happened? Not hurt, are you? Only frightened? Well, there's nothing to be afraid of now. Thank God we found you before you had time to come to any harm!"

"It's an ill wind that blows nobody any good," observed Dimsie sagely later on, when they were back in the safe sur-roundings of the junior sitting-room. "Guess what—we actually found Sylvia's note-book, Rosamund! I told you I'd do my best for you, but I don't mind confessing now that I hadn't much hope. You could have knocked me down with half a feather when I saw it lying there on the floor of the cave."

"Dimsie! On the floor of the cave!" cried Rosamund excitedly. "How in all the world did it get there? It—it must be a magic place!"

There was a shout of laughter from the others, and Rosamund grew pink with confusion.

"Magic, indeed!" jeered Winnie Hatton. "I believe she thinks there really are fairies and witches, and enchantments! You *are* a little stupid, Rosamund Garth!"

"She's nothing of the kind!" flared up Dimsie indignantly. "It was the most magical thing I've ever known to see that book lying in the middle of a secret cave. I should have been forced to believe in enchantments myself if Sylvia hadn't explained it when I took the book to her just now."

"Why, what did she say?" asked the rest with much interest, crowding round the speaker, who was seated on the edge of the table swinging her legs.

"Well, there was a queer crack just above us. Pam noticed it, and said she had often dropped stones down it, and Sylvia says she and Primrose were sitting beside that crack on the thunderstorm day when she sprained her ankle, so she thinks p'raps when they jumped up in a hurry the book may have fallen through. You see, Rosamund, it would never have been found if Pam and I hadn't lost ourselves."

Rosamund heaved a sigh of relief.

"Well, I'm ever so grateful to you for being lost, then," she said. "That book has been a terrible weight on my mind, and now not even Nita Tomlinson can say I'd anything to do with it.

But I'm more glad still," she added fervently, "that you and Pamela were found."

"So am I," added Erica. "All the time we were hunting for them I kept thinking how awful it would be if we only found their bones, and wondering what poor Miss Yorke would say to their mothers."

"They wouldn't have turned into bones as soon as all that," argued Jean Gordon. "They'd only have been corpses."

"Well, that would have been just as awkward for Miss Yorke," maintained Erica.

"I'm glad it wasn't awkward for her, then," exclaimed Pamela impulsively. "I've always respected Miss Yorke, but I never knew how much I liked her till she and Eric came hurrying down that passage today and found us."

"I know," assented Dimsie earnestly. "We've often thought her strict and fussy, but I don't think we've made enough allowance for her. After all, how would anybody like to be headmistress of Jane's with us for juniors?"

# CHAPTER 24

# THE VOTE OF
# THE SCHOOL

*"A meeting of the Upper and Middle Schools is called for eight o'clock this evening, in the assembly hall. Please arrange practising, etc., so that you will be able to be present.     (Signed)    Sylvia Drummond."*

This notice, put up at midday on Tuesday, was the result of a consultation overnight between Miss Yelland and Sylvia.

"I can't help it, my dear," said the games-mistress, looking worried. "If I had been in, and Nita had come to me with this project, I should have refused to hold it next Saturday for two reasons – first, because of the junior match, and, secondly, because none of you have been practising for water sports this term. After all, the bay is a public place, and however quiet we try to keep it, a thing of this sort will be sure to attract spectators, and I don't want the school to make a fool of itself. I wonder Nita didn't think of that for herself, as I told her – but she had everything cut and dried and the official notice up before I got home on Sunday evening."

"But, Miss Yelland, the date of the match has been fixed for ages," urged Sylvia. "Can't you say that the water sports must be on a later date? Surely *you* can override Nita, even though we can't!"

Miss Yelland shook her head regretfully.

"My dear girl, you forget she acted on Miss Yorke's authority."

"But Miss Yorke didn't know," persisted Sylvia eagerly. "She can cancel her consent if you explain matters to her. Do, Miss Yelland! She's awfully good about understanding awkward situations."

"I quite agree," assented the games-mistress heartily, having a very sincere admiration for her superior, "but, unfortunately, I *have* talked it over with her, and she – she doesn't see how she can alter matters now."

Miss Yelland spoke rather lamely, and clear-sighted Sylvia grasped the difficulty at once. Miss Yorke's rule was wise and beneficial, but she had a thing about keeping all her girls in their "proper place" relative to each other. Therefore, she could see no reason why an unimportant junior match should be allowed to stand in the way of a much bigger event wherein the whole of Jane's was to participate. At the same time, she was strictly just, and had said at once that, if the Lower School's match was down on the school fixture card for that date, then the other must be postponed. Miss Yelland had sent for the fixture card, which was in Nita's keeping, and discovered that half-term Saturday was blank.

"And that naturally settled it with Miss Yorke," she finished, having explained matters so far to Sylvia.

"Of course!" sighed the headgirl bitterly. "If Primrose hadn't been taken ill, she'd have seen the date was properly booked up on the card, but the arrangements were turned over to Nita, and then . . . ."

She stopped abruptly, conscious that she was putting her foot in it, seeing that it was Miss Yelland who had given these same arrangements into Nita's charge; but the junior mistress put the slip down to a very natural irritation, for she knew what pains Sylvia, as well as Primrose, had taken over the Lower School cricket.

"There's only one thing you can do now," she suggested. "Ask the school to vote on it. If you can tell Miss Yorke that the majority want the water sports postponed, she will certainly consent."

"I know," rejoined Sylvia gloomily, "but will they? Some of the others think the sports would get it."

"You can try, anyhow," said Miss Yelland. "Appeal to their sense of fair play. After all, it will be evident to most of them that Nita is selfish and unsporting in wishing to spoil the little ones' fun. For some reason, she has set herself against this team of theirs from the beginning. I can't imagine why."

"I can, though!" Sylvia assured herself grimly, as she went off to her study to write out her summons.

Mabs Hunter was, of course, among the first to read it, on her way back to the Lower Fourth room after music lesson. She rejoined her form absolutely bursting with news, as they could see at a glance, and it was hard on all concerned that Miss Edgar at the moment was taking them for geography; there was no possibility of whispering under "Teddy's" eagle eye, and Mabs's news had to wait.

The moment morning school was over the information came out with a rush.

"Sylvia's called a meeting, for eight o'clock tonight, of everybody except us and the Third Form. It must be about next Saturday."

For, of course, the juniors knew only too well of the jeopardy in which their match stood.

"Good old Sylvia!" cried Jean warmly. "She'll make that Nita change the date if anyone can! But I wonder why she wants a big meeting like that before she does it?"

"I'm going to find out," said Mabs determinedly. "I shall hide in the gym cupboard . . ."

A howl of indignation arose from her classmates at this suggestion, for the gym cupboard (where badminton nets, rackets, etc., were stocked) opened off the assembly hall.

"Eavesdropper!" cried Dimsie hotly. "And you call yourself an Anti-Soppist!"

"Well, I don't see why not," persisted Mabs, in whom there was a strong vein of obstinacy. "Sylvia hasn't forbidden any juniors to go to her meeting. She just hasn't invited them."

"Then go honestly, and sit down where she can see you," retorted Pam. "If you think she doesn't mind, why hide in the gym cupboard?"

"Yes," said Erica, "you know she doesn't want any of us, and that's the truth of it! I must say we're all surprised at you, Mabs Hunter, and I hope you won't give us cause to be so much surprised again."

Punctually at eight o'clock that evening, Sylvia entered the assembly hall and made her way to the platform at the upper end, on which stood a big table. She saw, to her satisfaction, that the Upper and Middle Schools had all turned out, every last one of them. They had some inkling of what she wanted to say to them, for the day chosen by Miss Yorke for the water fête had caused some comment among the girls, and they already guessed that Nita had "wangled" it for reasons of her own.

"Listen, girls," began Sylvia, speaking to them in the simple direct fashion which made her popular with her schoolfellows, "I've called this meeting because I want to appeal to you on behalf of the juniors. Most of you know how hard they've worked at their cricket all this term and how keen they are on the match which was to have been played next Saturday – their one and only match this summer, poor little beggars! Everybody understood it was fixed for Saturday – isn't that true, Margaret Hunter? You're captaining the Middle School side against them, aren't you?"

Margaret nodded from her seat in the background.

"I thought it was settled for half-term Saturday," she admitted.

"Well," Sylvia went on, leaning over the big desk, "through some – carelessness – the date was not entered on the fixture card, and in consequence this particular day has been selected for the water sports, about which I know you're all jolly keen – I am, myself; but if we have it on Saturday the junior match must be washed out altogether, for we all know there isn't another free holiday this term; something has been fixed up for each one of them."

"What about Monday?" suggested someone in the front row.

"Three of their best players are going home for Sunday and Monday; so are half of Margaret's team. For that matter, why not Monday for the sports?"

A loud shout of protest went up on all sides.

"Oh, no, Sylvia! Half the school's going off for the week-end by the evening train on Saturday. Nita said the fête was to be held in the morning because of that."

"So was the kids' match," Sylvia pointed out.

"But Miss Yorke knew that, and she gave her consent to the water fête."

"She didn't know, at the time she gave her consent," replied Sylvia, forbearing to add that Nita might easily have told her, "and afterwards she couldn't take it back, because it would be disappointing the majority for the sake of the few. But I think, myself, that she didn't realize the junior match had been properly settled up, because it hadn't been entered among the school fixtures. Anyhow, I went to see her just now, to tell her I'd called this meeting, and she says she will abide by the vote of the school. I rather fancy," Sylvia added, with a smile, "that she wants to give us the chance of being unselfish off our own bats. So it's for you to say whether we're going to be fair about it or not."

She had come to the end of her speech, and Nita, who had listened and watched in silence up till now, got on her feet.

"I never heard so much sentimental nonsense in all my . . ." she was beginning, when suddenly, with one brief preliminary knock, the door at the end of the long room flew open, and in burst Dimsie Maitland, clad gorgeously in a bright green kimono covered with laden branches of golden oranges, interspersed with weird and wonderful birds never seen on land or sea.

"Oh, Sylvia, I'm awfully sorry," she panted, "but I had to interrupt you, 'cause if I hadn't you might have been much more upset than you can possibly be with me."

After which cryptic utterance she flashed, kingfisher-like, across the hall and dived into the big gymnasium cupboard on the other side. There was a startled squeal, a clatter of falling rackets, and the kingfisher emerged again in righteous wrath, dragging Mabs Hunter, red-cheeked and dusty.

"After all we said to you about it this afternoon, too!" stormed Dimsie, punctuating her remarks with angry shakes. "Nobody thought you'd have *dared* till we found you missing at bedtime! How often has Erica told you that curiosity killed the cat! Now you've really gone and done it!"

"I haven't!" protested Mabs feebly. "I – I – haven't! D-don't be so – so rough!"

"Yes you have! You've stooped to the darkest depths, so don't make it worse by denying it! I'm very sorry, Sylvia and everybody, but you can see for yourselves it's better to be interrrupted than to be eavesdropped upon."

"Much," agreed Sylvia, with a frantic effort after self-control and a proper severity, but it was no use. The meeting, which had been irritable and inclined to sulkiness, suddenly gave way completely, and peals of laughter rang out from even the sedatest prefects. Sylvia herself clung to the table in a soundless agony of mirth, while even Nita Tomlinson laughed with the rest.

"I don't see anything funny about it," ejaculated the shocked Dimsie, staring at them with reproachful eyes, and feeling that this outbreak would have a very bad moral effect on the wicked Mabs. "Of course, if you think it's *amusing* to listen in cupboards . . ."

"We don't," said Sylvia hastily, as she pulled herself together and mopped her streaming eyes. "Nobody was laughing at that, so please don't think so. I – I shan't attempt to tell Mabs what we think of her, because she knows only too well, and in any case I believe I can safely leave it to her room-mates. Take her upstairs to Erica, Dimsie – she's your monitress, isn't she? – and tell her what I've said."

Dimsie waited no second bidding, but hauled her captive off before there should be any more unseemly mirth to spoil the effect of the headgirl's words, and as the door closed behind them Phyllis Heathley rose to her feet.

"I've got a proposal to make, Sylvia," she said, "and I hope everybody will agree to it. Instead of interfering with the Babes' Eleven on Saturday, let's wash out the match between the Sixth Form and the Fifth and have the water sports on that day instead. We all get enough cricket anyway, and it would give us more time to work up our swimming."

"Marvellous idea, Phyl!" cried Sylvia heartily. "Those of you who agree, please put up your hands."

The school hailed the proposal with relief as the easiest way out of the dificulty. Every hand but Nita's promptly went up, and seeing this she, too, at length lifted hers grudgingly.

"Carried unanimously!" exclaimed Sylvia, with a sigh of relief. "Thanks awfully, girls. I'll tell Miss Yorke straight away, and Miss Yelland will see about altering the fixture card."

# CHAPTER 25

# TRUTH WILL
# OUT

Next day Primrose Garth was out of quarantine, though Matron did not want her to begin work again till after half-term. Primrose herself felt languid and depressed, and seemed to shrink alike from the thought of work or play. She took her hammock down through the wood, and slinging it to a branch of the old twisted cedar, ensconced herself with a book and some fancy work to while the afternoon away.

"I believe the girl would be better with her regular occupations," said Miss Yelland, watching from the terrace, for idleness in any shape or form irritated her.

Matron, however, shook her head.

"She must get her strength back first," she answered wisely. "That was a bad attack she had, and moreover, Primrose has been mopey and unlike herself all this term. Mabs Hunter, is that you?"

"Yes, Matron," responded Mabs, pausing in full flight along the terrace.

"Then find Meg Flynn and tell her from me that Primrose is out of quarantine now, and she'll find her somewhere down in the wood. Perhaps that will do it," added Matron to herself, as she turned back into the house.

Mabs found Meg tidying her desk in the Sixth Form room, and delivered her message, after which she lingered for a moment.

"I say, Meg," she volunteered, "I know some awfully interesting news."

"Do you?" asked Meg, with no great display of interest.

"Yes. I'm just going to tell Erica and the others. They'll be

126

awfully pleased, but I'm afraid you won't."

"Perhaps not," assented Meg, piling her books neatly in order. Mabs felt piqued that her usual method for arousing curiosity was proving unsuccessful.

"You'll never guess!" she said enticingly.

"Then I shan't bother to try," returned Meg, yawning and stretching herself.

Mabs looked distinctly crestfallen.

"Then I suppose I shall have to tell you," she said in disappointed tones. "Margaret told me, 'cause she sleeps in her dormitory, and she read the letter aloud when they went up to make their beds after breakfast. Nita Tomlinson is going to leave at the end of this term and go to a school in France!"

"Thank you," said Meg, unmoved. "So she told me herself at breakfast. One of these days, Mabs, my child, you'll find yourself grown up into a horrid little gossip."

Mabs hopped agitatedly on one foot, holding the other in her hand.

"Don't you mind a bit?" she queried in an aggrieved voice.

"Not a bit," responded the senior placidly, "so you'd better cut along and tell your little pals. I've no doubt they'll be excited enough to please even you."

After Mabs had gone Meg finished her task, then went in search of her broad-brimmed sun hat, and betook herself down the wood path which led to the twisted cedar, and as she went she whistled "The Minstrel Boy" with a note of jubilation which had been missing lately from this forbidden form of music.

"Meg! Meg!" cried Mademoiselle, passing her with a shake of the head. "*Ce n'est pas comme il faut, mon enfant.*"

Meg laughed naughtily.

"Sure, I couldn't be *comme il faut,* Mademoiselle, if I tried for a month of Sundays," she declared, " and I'm not trying today."

Leaving the path, she took a short cut downwards, leaping from step to step of the tree roots, and landing finally in the tiny glade where Primrose was swinging herself listlessly, her long blonde hair tumbling across the hamock. Meg's greeting was casual – perhaps she could not trust herself for anything else.

"Those tresses of yours looks very picturesque, you know," she said, "but you'll catch it if Miss Yorke sees you with it loose."

For Miss Yorke decreed that long hair should always be pinned up off the face.

"No, I shan't – I'm still an invalid," rejoined Primrose, but her eyes lit up with a flash of pleasure, and she smiled at Meg. "It's quite safe to talk to me. Matron says I haven't got a germ left."

"And you're really feeling better?" asked Meg, flopping on the pine needles below her.

"Yes, I think so – at least, I suppose I shall soon. Tell me what's been happening. We lost the match with Westover High School?"

"Yes, and everybody says it was owing to your being out of it – everybody except Nita, I mean. Look here, Prim – I can't beat about the bush – I've got to tell you, anyhow – I'm simply fed up with Nita Tomlinson! She isn't a bit what I took her for."

"I've never liked her," said Primrose slowly. A certain delicacy withheld her from giving any stronger opinion against her rival.

"I know, and I wish I'd listened to you . . . But she seemed such a good sport, and she was keen on the things I liked. Thinking things over these last few days, I can see that the mask kept slipping, but she has something mesmerizing about her, and I just closed my eyes to her faults. She's not straight, Primrose, and now that I've found her out I can't stick it!"

"But how did you find her out?" asked Primrose with interest.

Meg hesitated.

"It's strictly confidential, of course, but I don't see why I shouldn't tell you. Anyhow, I shall, so here goes!"

Hugging her knees to her chin and watching her friend's face with some anxiety the while, Meg told her tale of what had happened on Saturday at the club.

"You see, it never entered my head that Miss Yorke didn't know, and all the time Nita had deceived her, too. You can't think how uncomfortable I feel, Primrose, because I can't go and own up without giving her away as well, and she won't let me."

"It's horribly awkward for you," admitted Primrose, knitting her brows. "That's the worst of getting mixed up with girls like Nita Tomlinson – you can't unmix yourself when you discover what they're really like."

Meg picked up a fallen cone and shied it at a distant rabbit twinkling between the tree trunks.

"That isn't all," she went on sheepishly. "I've been such a pig to you ever since I started going round with Nita. I've felt rotten about it all the time, but somehow – I don't know what it is about that girl, but if you're friends with her, you seem forced to drop everybody else."

Primrose nodded.

"I was so afraid you might think me jealous," she began, but Meg interrupted her by jumping up suddenly and giving her an impulsive hug.

"You weren't! You've been a lamb – and I know quite well how it was, though I can't explain it. You would never have cared an atom if I'd been pally with Daph, or Sylvia, or the Heathleys."

"I don't think I should," assented Primrose, returning the hug with rapture. "And then, you see, Meg, Nita was so awfully good at games, and I am no use at anything but cricket. I knew how much that sort of thing meant to you, and the reason why I took such pains with those juniors was to – to try and show you I wasn't such a clown as you thought."

"I never thought you were a clown!" cried Meg hotly. "In fact I . . ."

"Meg Flynn! Hey, Meg! Are you there? Miss Yorke wants you."

Hilda Heathley's voice was wafted from somewhere above them, and in response to Meg's answering call she came hurriedly through the bracken.

"You're to go to her in her study at once – you and Nita Tomlinson. I believe you're in for the row of a lifetime," added Hilda encouragingly. "Miss Yorke looked as black as thunder. Hullo, Primrose! Better?"

Meg turned away with a meaning grimace.

"The secret's out!" she exclaimed. "Sure, and I'm not sorry!"

Outside the door of Miss Yorke's study Nita was waiting for her with an air of defiance which masked some nervousness. There was only one person in the whole school whom Nita feared, and that person was the headmistress.

The two girls knocked at the door, and crept in with furtive glances at Miss Yorke, which showed them that Hilda's description had not been exaggerated. Her brows were drawn together in a sharp frown and her lips compressed, while before her on the table lay a copy of *The Westover Weekly News*.

*"Come in, girls," she said in freezing tones. "Perhaps you will kindly tell me what is the meaning of this."*

*She pointed to a paragraph in the paper, and, following her finger with guilty eyes, Meg and Nita read:—*

### *"OPEN COMPETITION AT ST ELSTRITH'S TENNIS CLUB*

*"This annual event passed off with great success on a day of brilliant sunshine and soft breezes. At two-thirty precisely," etc., etc.*

Their eyes ran hurriedly down the short column of print, and alighted on their own names.

*"The laurels of the afternoon rested with the bright young champions of the Jane Willard Foundation, Miss Magdalen Flynn and Miss Juanita Tomlinson, who held their own with considerable adroitness against all comers."*

A few words of praise about their play and prophecies of future triumphs for the school they represented closed the account. Meg looked up and met Miss Yorke's gaze with a very red face, but her eyes were honest.

"It's quite true, Miss Yorke. We did play, and – and I'm very sorry about it."

"You went, in deliberate defiance of my wishes, and played at this club – two seniors! and you, Meg, a prefect!"

Meg remained silent, but Nita suddenly raised her head, and spoke with her pertest expression.

"You needn't blame Meg, Miss Yorke, for she thought all the time that we had your permission, or she would never have gone. I told her I'd asked you, and she didn't know that I'd only asked leave for us to go to tea at Miss Austin's. She wanted to come to you and own up when she heard the truth, but I wouldn't let her, because I didn't see why we should get into a row unnecessarily. Now that you've found us out, of course, it makes a difference."

"Yes, Nita," said Miss Yorke with ominous quietness, "I think you will find that it makes a great difference."

# CHAPTER 26

# "THE BABES' ELEVEN"

The day of "the" match had arrived at last, and the junior team heaved a sigh of relief at the settled appearance of the sky. On Thursday night it had rained; Friday had seemed undecided, but there was no doubt about Saturday's weather, and Miss Yelland, tapping the barometer in the hall as they went out from breakfast, announced that it was rising steadily.

"Really," said Dimsie, shaking her curls, "we've had so many problems lately that I shan't feel safe till we actually go on to the field – though I don't see what could happen to prevent us now."

"Oh, nothing – nothing!" cried Pam, with a little skip of glee. "The only trouble is how we can pass the time till ten o'clock."

"Those of you who are going away this evening can spend it in packing your suitcases," remarked the matron's repressive tones behind them. "The rest must go and keep out of mischief somewhere."

"That's me," sighed Dimsie, whose home was in Scotland, and who had no outlying relations nearer than Birkenhead. The Maitlands always spent their half-term holidays at Jane's, but nevertheless managed to enjoy themselves very well.

Ten o'clock found the Babes' Eleven grouped nervously round the pavilion, while the Middle School team, with lofty unconcern, sat about the steps or grass and discussed the rival merits of their bats.

"Now, then," said Joyce Lamond briskly as the hour chimed faintly from the church clock at St Elstrith-on-the-Downs, "I'll toss, Jean, and you call."

"Heads!" said Jean earnestly, and instantly wondered whether "Tails" would have brought her better luck.

"It's tails," responded the prefect. "Go on, Margaret, you've won the toss. Now, Jean, get your fielders out, and put Betty Grey where she won't get catches to drop: that's what she usually does, as you know. Daphne is going to umpire for you, and I'm acting for the Middle School."

Now that the actual moment had come, a sort of desperate coolness fell upon Jean. She no longer feared her responsibilities as captain, but placed her followers with a careful discretion which caused Miss Yelland to remark to Sylvia, in some amusement, that Jean had all the qualities of a capable commander.

"She's pretty smart for a junior," assented Sylvia. "We'll have her playing for Jane's one of these days – which you'll be here to see, Miss Yelland, but I shan't."

Miss Yelland laughed.

"It seems impossible to picture Jane's without you, Sylvia," she said, with a teasing smile. "One can scarcely realize that this term is your last."

Margaret Hunter had gone out first to bat, taking Madge Anderson with her. Both had been known to give a good account of themselves at the wicket; but if the juniors were nervous today, their opponents erred on the side of over-confidence. Perhaps it was owing to this that Madge suddenly found herself out for a duck; Pamela bowled, Joan Hardy stumped. The shock sobered Margaret and caused Madge's successor to play more carefully than she had, perhaps, intended; it also had a very reassuring effect on the shaky juniors.

Margaret and her new partner now settled down to a comfortable stand, which nothing seemed able to shake, and the score on the board steadily rose by twos and threes. Jean, who was beginning to look anxious again, finally took the ball herself; she had been watching Margaret's strokes with painful attention during the last over, and an idea had come to her. After sending down three orthodox overarm balls, which Margaret cheerfully patted away for a couple of runs apiece, she suddenly fired off a swift underarm one, and before Margaret knew where she was the bails lay about her on the grass.

"That," commented Joyce Lamond, joining lazily in the

applause from the pavilion, "may be termed strategy."

Whatever it was, it had given Jean confidence. With flushed cheeks and sparkling eyes she awaited Ursula Grey, who took Margaret's place at the wicket, and made a single on the last ball of the over, thus bringing herself face to face with the bowling once more. Then in her next over Jean did it again. Just as Ursula felt she was getting her hand in, in came a swift underarm ball, and the bails flew.

"Go it, Jean!" shrieked Dimsie joyously from the rough grass at the side of the field where she and Mabs had established themselves. "That's three of their men out for twenty-one. Play up, Lower School!"

"There's Evelyn Thomas going out to bat now," observed Mabs with a fine contempt. "She's simply rotten! Margaret must have thought she needn't bother about us when she picked old Evelyn!"

Mabs was feeling more like herself than she had done since Tuesday evening, for her room-mates had (as Sylvia expected) dealt faithfully with her in the matter of the gym cupboard. Not only had they refused to listen to any of the valuable information she had picked up while there, but Erica had sternly passed a sentence of silence upon her, and she had not been allowed to utter a word of any sort while in the dormitory until that morning. Mabs, who loved above all things the sound of her own prattle, nearly wept, especially when downstairs (where she might talk) the Anti-Soppists forbade her to mention cricket. Her punishment was all the harder because the others never scrupled to discuss the important match before her, nor what they believed to have happened at the meeting she had attended in hiding. Their conjectures were so very wide of the truth that it was agony to Mabs to listen when she might not correct them.

And Erica had made an addition to the rules of their society. It ran as follows:

"No Anti-Soppist may at any time hide in cupboards or under tables or any other place of concealment to hear things that aren't meant for her, no matter how important they may be to the society."

It was a rule which Mabs was not likely to break soon

again; but today she felt she had served her sentence, expiated her crime, and become at peace with her little world once more.

"I told you so!" she exclaimed triumphantly, when a straight delivery of Jean's found Evelyn's middle stump. "Oh, Dimsie, we *are* coming on!"

But Dimsie clutched her arm, opening her eyes wide with excitement.

"Do you know what's happened?" she exclaimed in tones of awe. "Jean's done the hat-trick!"

The school cheered lustily at the junior captain's exploit, while Mabs and Dimsie yelled themselves hoarse. Only, when silence reigned once more and Rosamund Garth had been put on to bowl to Evelyn's successor, Mabs said doubtfully:

"Are you quite sure it was a hat-trick? Don't you have to take three wickets, one after the other, for no runs, or something of that sort? Margaret and Ursula both made runs."

"It was a kind of hat-trick," said Dimsie firmly, "and a jolly fine one too!"

The tail of the Middle School team did better than their captain had dared to hope. Perhaps they felt themselves on their mettle against these juniors who had been so much under-rated. At any rate, they were all out for ninety-seven in the end, which had not seemed probable at one stage.

"Now it's us!" said Jean in a voice which shook more from excitement than fear this time, as their opponents went out to field. "I'm going to put myself in first wicket down, 'cause I'm not as good as Pam or Winnie. You two go in first, and listen if you must come out, don't let it be because you've given away catches."

Those people at Jane's who had taken no interest in the juniors' cricket practice were astonished to see how well the first pair shaped at the wicket.

Pamela's play was rash almost to wildness, but it gave promise of brilliancy in the future, and even now her daring strokes had better results than seemed possible from their riski-ness. She left the pitch with fifteen to her credit, including two boundaries, when Madge Anderson stumped her.

"You always keep me on the jumps when you're batting, Pam," Dimsie declared, "but somehow it comes all right in the end. And just look at Winnie – she thinks she's there for the rest of the day!"

Winnie's stolid little figure certainly had a very set appearance as she calmly defended her end, only taking safe runs, and driving so hard that the runs were very often safe. Between them, she and Jean brought the score up to thirty-three before the latter had to return to the pavilion, clean bowled by Margaret Hunter.

"Thirty-three for two wickets!" cried Dimsie. "That's more than they got for three. Hey, Mabs! Your sister can sure bowl!"

"That was the twister which got her into the second eleven," said Mabs with pardonable pride. "You going in, Betty? Remember – don't give away a catch!"

The caution was justified. Poor Betty failed to break her duck, and Joan Hardy, who followed her, managed to run the rock-like Winnie out. Four men gone and the score still under forty! Jean felt a trifle dizzy as she sent Erica out to join the erratic Joan. It seemed, however, that Joan had had a shock. She took no more risks, and Erica, hitting harder than her side had believed possible, made nineteen runs before Ursula caught her in the slips.

"Just as well for you, Eric, that you made a tidy score," was Jean's greeting as she returned, hot and crestfallen. "There's something so disgraceful about sending catches."

"I know," assented Erica, with the most surprising meekness. "And nineteen is such an untidy sort of score."

The morning was growing steadily hotter, with only a faint breeze from the sea, which hardly reached them in the sheltered valley-bottom where the playing field lay. The onlookers herded themselves together in such shade as could be found, and the fielders pulled their broad-brimmed hats lower down on their brows. Jean's heart was beginning to sink, for the figures on the board stood at only sixty-nine, and her best bats were all out.

"Never mind if you are beaten now," said Primrose Garth kindly. "You've put up a better fight than anyone believed possible."

"But we're not going to be beaten," declared Dimsie

positively. "Cheer up, Jean and put Rosamund in next. It's wonderful, sometimes, how she'll rise to the occasion."

"Well," said Jean resignedly, "she'll either do that or she'll burst out crying. Go in after Edith Milne, Ros, and don't you come out till we've squashed them!"

Rosamund's strong point was bowling; she had never before distinguished herself with the bat, and possibly only the loyal Dimsie had hopes now of her saving the situation. At any rate, she took her stand before Margaret's bowling with a sort of desperate courage, and tried hard to remember all she had ever learnt of cricket at home or at school, only to find her mind a perfect blank.

The first ball was contemptuously easy; Rosamund made two runs off it, and this seemed to reassure her wonderfully. She hit cautiously for the first over, then, as nothing dreadful happened, she became more confident and hit out.

"Not bad!" breathed Dimsie from the pavilion steps. "I told you she'd play up all right. That's eight – there! ten – Jean, we'll do it yet!"

Rosamund afterwards accounted for her own success by the fact that the heat, which made Margaret and her bowlers limp, only livened her up and caused her to feel more brisk. The pitch was hard and the ball fast, but still she hit it, and kept on hitting. One of her partners was bowled for four, the next made six, and was out l.b.w. Rosamund realized, in an absent sort of way, that the last man was in, and that she was a very small "man", who would probably make nought, and that it would now depend on her alone to go on scoring. Jean hoped it of her, Dimsie expected it; she was less optimistic herself, but – she went on scoring.

The Middle School bowler pulled herself together and sent down a tremendously fast ball, straight for Rosamund's middle stump, but it met her bat instead. There was a terrific crack, a moment's breathless hush, and then cheer after cheer went up from Jane's. Rosamund had got a boundary and the Babes' score stood at ninety-nine!

The next ball passed her guard.

"And that," said Joyce Lamond, later on, "was the kid you wanted to scrap, Nita! By the way, what made you change your mind so suddenly?"

Nita did not deign to reply, but Meg grinned maliciously.

"Force of circumstances," she suggested. "Anyhow, Primrose, allow me to congratulate you on the result of your labours. The Babes' Eleven did you proud."

# CHAPTER 27

# THE A.S.S. OUT
# OF THE BAG

Half-term Saturday was drawing to its close in a blaze of glory for the junior eleven. They had fully justified their existence beyond their wildest dreams: that morning they had not only faced but defeated the Middle School!

"Of course," said Margaret Hunter, "we only put up a scratch team against them. It seemed a pity to discourage the poor little things in their very first match, or else we could have beaten them easily enough."

At which the juniors grinned impishly and nudged each other and winked, for their victory remained, nevertheless, an accomplished fact, and Miss Yorke herself had congratulated them.

Erica had summoned a meeting of the Anti-Soppists in their council chamber at five o'clock, and there they gathered punctually, all except Dimsie Maitland, who was nowhere to be seen.

"Well, we can't wait for her any longer," observed Erica impatiently, when ten minutes had passed without result. "Take your flower-pots, friends, and the meeting shall be declared open."

"Meetings don't open – only bazaars," objected Jean, the argumentative.

"They do," contradicted Erica. "I've often heard of meetings opening with prayer."

"Yes, but they're the missionary sort, and ours is – ours is political."

"Look here, Jean Gordon," said Erica in her most repressive tones, "are you the eldest in this society, or am I? Besides, you oughtn't to be lifting up your voice quite so much when you've been the one to get us into a fix.''

Jean subsided.

"I only tried to keep the rules," she muttered.

"Yes, but you kept them tactlessly, and you might have known better after Miss Moffatt gave us 'Tact' for our essay subject last week.''

"What did she do?" inquired Rosamund Garth, who had not heard the full history of Jean's transgression.

"Do?" said Erica. "Well, you know Jean's parents sent her a huge bunch of pink roses for her birthday yesterday? She'd just fetched them from the front hall when she bumped into Miss Phipps – you know Pips went away last night for half-term – and she had on her best dress (that lovely floaty one), and she asked Jean to give her one of her pink rosebuds to wear, and Jean told her she couldn't!''

"Never!" cried Rosamund, round-eyed with horror. "Whatever did Pips say?''

"Well, what was I to do?" protested Jean indignantly. "You've made screeds of rules now, but you know one of the very first was about giving flowers to mistresses and seniors.''

"Yes, but there's no need to be rude about it," Erica pointed out, "'specially when your arms were absolutely crammed with roses under her very nose! That's what I mean about tact. You might have said, 'Please help yourself, Miss Phipps, and take whichever you like best.' Then there would have been no unpleasantness.''

"Miss Phipps was tactful, though," said Mabs Hunter, with admiration. "She just said, 'Oh, I see! Your hands are too full, are they? Never mind – I daresay I can get one from the garden,' and off she went.''

"But worse than that happened afterwards," continued Erica, "because some of the Upper Second were passing, and they stopped and asked Jean why she had been so grudging to poor old Pips, and teased her about being Scottish and mean (which is all wrong of course – I'm Scottish myself) and Jean got into a rage and said she belonged to a secret society, and was bound by its rules not to go giving flowers to people, and they asked her what the society was, and she said the A.S.S.!''

"And you can just fancy how those big girls jeered!" finished Mabs, who – needless to say – had been an eye-witness of the scene.

"Well," said Jean, scarlet and shamefaced, "I was coming out of my rage a wee bit then, and I thought I'd told them too much, and you mightn't like it if I gave them the real full name; and societies are always called by initials, and those *are* the initials of ours."

"We'll never hear the end of it!" said Pam Hughes gloomily. "I expect everybody in Jane's knows it now, and Ursula Grey called out 'Come on, you A.S.S.!' to Rosamund this morning."

"She *did* come on, though," declared Erica, "and that's one reason why I called this meeting tonight. Friends and sisters" – assuming her official tone – "we are met here together this evening mostly to congratulate ourselves on having played and won the match – no! don't cheer for half a minute – and because two members of our society have distinguished themselves greatly. Jean Gordon has almost (but not quite) wiped out the memory of her awful *foot pas* yesterday evening by getting a hat-trick . . ." (loud and irrepressible cheers) "and the hat-trick is the hat-trick, even if it *is* against three of the rottenest bats in the Middle School. As for Rosamund Garth . . ." (renewed cheers) "besides bowling jolly well, which was only what we expected of her, she actually made twenty, not out, and very considerably helped to win the match."

The hearty applause which followed drowned the noise of footsteps approaching at a run, and everybody jumped when the rickety door burst suddenly open and the missing Dimsie bounced into their midst.

"You'll never guess what!" she cried, half-strangling Rosamund in a bear-like embrace. "Miss Yelland has been to Miss Yorke and told her that good old Ros has been trying her hardest at lessons lately, and Miss Yorke says she's to be moved up straight away into the Lower Fourth! Only she'll have to go on sleeping in the junior dormitory till the end of the term, but she's Lower Fourth all right, at last – isn't it absolutely terrific?"

Renewed congratulations were showered on Rosamund from all sides, till she felt quite sore with the repeated and vigorous thumps which descended on her shoulders.

"It's all Dimsie's doing," she said modestly. "I'd never have been able to learn my lessons if Dimsie hadn't shown me every evening; and it was jolly good of her, 'cause she might have been practising at the nets all that time, and Sylvia Drummond said today that, if only Dimsie had taken pains and practised more, she'd have been in the junior eleven instead of Joan Hardy."

"Oh no, not me!" protested Dimsie, much embarrassed, but Rosamund was bent on singing her friend's praises.

"And I'd never have got into the eleven myself," she continued, "if Dimsie hadn't stood up to that hateful Nita and simply made her put my name back. Miss Yorke knows all about it now, so I should think we can tell you what happened, shouldn't you, Dimsie?"

"I don't think it matters now," assented Dimsie. "If there's anything I'm thankful for, it is that we've only got half a term more of Nita Tomlinson!"

So Rosamund told her story, and the Anti-Soppists listened with fervent interest till she had finished, when Erica exclaimed:

"I bet there's no one to beat you for cheek, Dimsie Maitland, in the whole of Jane's! Fancy threatening a senior like that – captain of games too!"

"Well, it had to be done," said Dimsie. "I didn't exactly mean to be cheeky, you know."

"You never do," groaned Erica. "Not that I care what you say to Nita Tomlinson, but when people get into habits they can't always get out of them, and suppose you did that sort of thing to Sylvia Drummond some day!"

"I shouldn't ever want to," returned Dimsie comfortably. "Sylvia isn't a sneak."

Here Mabs Hunter broke in, being oppressed with the fact that she had saved a piece of information all the afternoon in order that she might reveal it at the meeting.

"I know something awfully interesting," she remarked insinuatingly, looking round the circle; but Erica had lately been inspired as to a new way of dealing with the exasperating Mabs.

"I don't suppose you do, really," she rejoined. "It's probably something awfully stupid."

"It isn't!" cried Mabs hurriedly, falling into the trap. "It's about the secret passage, so there! I heard Miss Yorke and Miss Edgar talking about it when our side was waiting to go in. She's going to have all the old entrances in the grounds opened up, so that we can play hide-and-seek round the little short passages, but we're not to go down the long passage to the cave without permission, and it's going to be made into a sort of summer-house."

There was a chorus of approval from the rest of the society, who yearned to explore the passages, and had not yet been allowed to. Then Erica, stepping up on to her flowerpot, said:

"My young friends, before we bring this gathering to an end (and we'll have to soon, because it's time some of us were getting ready to catch the train), I want to propose an important amendation to you, in order to prevent the foolish jeering of people like the Upper Second. In future we shall be known as the Anti-Soppist League, and nobody can be the least funny about calling us A.S.L."

"Hear, hear!" clamoured the others, and Jean Gordon added, "I only wish you'd thought of it before."

"I can't be expected to think of everything at once," retorted Erica tartly. "By the way, Dimsie, I suppose you're quite sure that Rosamund has been moved up? You didn't just hear it the way Mabs hears things?"

"No, I know it's true," answered Dimsie simply. "That's why I was late for the meeting, 'cause I wanted to make quite sure, so I went and asked Miss Yorke."

Erica threw up her hands in despair.

"Well, of all the cheek!" she exclaimed.

# CHAPTER 28

# THE WATER
# SPORTS

Nobody knew what Miss Yorke had said to Nita Tomlinson regarding the matter of the St Elstrith tennis tournament; but on the Tuesday evening, when all who had been away for half-term had returned, it was publicly announced that Nita was deposed from her position, and for the rest of the term Meg Flynn would take her place as sports-captain. Which decree showed, of course, that Miss Yorke exonerated Meg from blame in the matter, though she spoke to her seriously in private about allowing herself to be so easily taken in.

Jane's had no idea of what Nita thought about her punishment, for she kept entirely to herself, seeming to realize how unpopular she had made herself with her school-fellows.

"I wouldn't be in Miss Yorke's shoes for anything," remarked Daphne Maitland, laughing. "Nita looks as though she were planning a very awful kind of vengeance for this piece of disgrace."

"Very probably," assented Sylvia. "Goodness knows I've no liking for Nita Tomlinson, but it must be pretty sickening to know she's got to take a back seat when all the return matches are coming on. In a way, you know, it's pretty valiant of her to go on playing. If she chose to go off in a huff, it would let Jane's down badly at games."

"I believe it's the one thing she cares about," observed Daphne thoughtfully. "And Meg has got the running of the water fête too."

"Responsibility will be jolly good for Meg," was Sylvia's rejoinder. "Are you entering for the seniors' race, Daph?"

"Yes – and the tubs. There ought to be several heats in

that – apparently half the school are down for it. My young cousin told me this morning she had entered."

The Lower Fourth were greatly excited over the water sports, and had put Dimsie forward as their champion for every event. Though she had never lived by the sea till she was sent to Jane's, Dimsie had taken to the water like a duck, and was quite the fastest swimmer in her form.

"Remember, you've got to win the tub race," Erica told her, as they changed together in a corner of the school bathing hut. "Pam and I put our names down for the fun of the thing, but we're no good. Pam might get the apple hunt – her mouth's larger than yours, but she can't swim as fast."

"I'll do what I can," Dimsie returned modestly; "but, of course, the big girls will win all the open races."

"I don't know about that," retorted Erica, following her out onto the sands. "Bigness isn't everything in a swimming competition."

The whole of Jane's seemed to have assembled on the tiny beach that afternoon. Even the mistresses were sitting on the rocks at the foot of the high white cliffs or in the shade of the breakwaters. In the middle of the little bay was a raft, tethered to the seabed in order to provide a diving platform, and often swarming with seagulls.

At present it swarmed with the Upper School, awaiting Miss Yelland's signal to race out to a marker buoy and back. The games-mistress, in a very fashionable swimsuit of poppy-red, sat on the edge of the tilted raft holding the rope of a small bell which hung from a wooden post behind her.

"Are you ready? A little further back there, Lesley! Nancy, your hands aren't right – that's it. Good. Are you r-ready? Go!"

The bell clanged. The tense row of girls shot outwards and down into the clear blue water. The rest of the school, crowding along the edge of the beach and the shallow water between it and the raft, yelled encouragement to their favourites.

"Go on, Sylvia! Get a move on, Joyce! Daph's leading – no, it's Phyllis! You can do it, Joyce – Sylvia – Joyce – Joyce – *Joyce!*"

"Joyce is in first," proclaimed Miss Yorke, who had been following the event through binoculars, "Sylvia and Phyllis second – a dead heat. Apparently Nita Tomlinson doesn't mean to exert herself this morning."

"Sulking," commented Miss Edgar tersely. "Nita's will be the one departure I shall not regret at the end of the term. A most disagreeable girl!"

"And yet she must have some good points," mused Miss Yorke doubtfully. "She is certainly keen for the school's advancement in games. Look, there go the little ones! Dear me! There should have been three batches for this race instead of two. What chance has a mite like Nora Blyth against that big, strong Evelyn Thomas?"

"Erica will get this," declared Miss Moffatt decidedly. "I back her staying power against any of them. Evelyn can never keep it up."

But the Anti-Soppists had not chosen their champion without knowledge. Dimsie got back to the raft first, with Erica close at her heels, and Jane's expressed its pleasure in ear-splitting yells. If anyone had told Dimsie that she was the most popular girl in the Lower School, she would have been very much astonished; but it was the truth, nevertheless, and when (with the help of a handicap) she won the dormitory race against Joyce Lamond the cliffs rang again with her ovations.

"You'd think it'd turn her head!" exclaimed Meg Flynn, as the cheers died down. "Any other kid would be unbearable after a little of this sort of thing."

"Oh, I don't know," said Daphne, trying to be unbiased. "Dimsie isn't the only sensible kid in the place, but she's not a bad little soul, I'm willing to admit. Come on, Meg! They're bringing out the tubs."

This item proved to be the most amusing on the programme. It started from the shore – the elder girls taking their turn first – and when they had pushed their half-barrels far enough out, they clambered gingerly in and seated themselves even more gingerly. Their paddles were bits of plywood begged from the school handyman, and roars of laughter went up from the spectators as fat Nancy Harriman, having capsized altogether, made violent but fruitless efforts to re-embark. Ursula Grey, with marvellous skill and ingenuity, paddled straight for the buoy with a curious wobbling motion which, Miss Yorke declared, it made her sea-sick to watch. In spite of being twice shipwrecked, Ursula managed to keep easily ahead of the others, and grounded in great spirits, having triumphed in public for the first time in her life.

"'Tisn't fair," protested Meg Flynn, laughing. "That swift destroyer of yours is far the most seaworthy. Mine couldn't think whether it was a submarine or a turtle, and in the end it bucked and threw me. Kids next! Come on, you lot!"

The Lower School had been looking forward all the morning to the tub race, and took possession of their craft with peals of joy, not in the least daunted by the fact that some of their elders had returned from the trip feeling decidedly sea-sick. Being much ligher the juniors balanced themselves more easily, and their catastrophes were fewer on the way out to the buoy. Owing to some peculiarity of their vessels, Dimsie and Erica were a little distance behind the others, but they stuck to it pluckily, hoping that the more successful navigators might yet come to grief, and allow the slowcoaches to overtake them in the end.

Dimsie, who was leading, had rounded the buoy and was heading shorewards once more, when Erica lost control of her tub, and somehow the two fouled one another and both capsized. The onlookers on beach and raft laughed and cheered ironically, as the two heads bobbed in the water, but gradually realized that something had gone wrong; one girl was trying to support the other, while a faint cry for help came across the narrow stretch of sea between. Several of the older girls at once plunged in from the shore, where they were gathered, but Miss Yelland was ahead of them. Like a red streak she shot through the water, and the others, seeing that they were not needed, hung back. Old Tom, the boatman, who should have been at hand with his skiff, had rowed some distance out to examine certain floats in which he was interested, and failed to see the agitated signals from the shore.

"What is it?" panted the games-mistress anxiously, as she reached the scene of the shipwreck. "Is Erica hurt?"

"I don't know," said Dimsie, gasping a little. "I think – she hit her head on the tub. Anyhow – she turned giddy – and she can't swim yet."

"I'll take over," said Miss Yelland peremptorily. "Keep still, Erica – you'll be all right in a minute. Now then! – I suppose you can manage, Dimsie? Nothing the matter with *your* head?"

"Oh, no, thanks!" answered Dimsie, breathing rather fast. "Take Eric – I'll hang on to the tub and rest a bit . . ."

She relinquished her charge with a sense of relief, hardly realizing how exhausted she had been by the fright and strain of the last few minutes. The tub had drifted a little, and she had hardly enough energy to go after it; she thought she would float for a minute or two, but what a rushing sound the sea was making in her ears! Those queer lights, too . . .

With a sensation of horror she realized that she was sinking, that she could not keep herself up, and there was nothing to hold on by. She gave one feeble half-strangled cry, and then went down – down . . .

She was coming up for the second time, when strong hands gripped her, and a voice, which even then she was astonished to recognize as Nita Tomlinson's, said briefly:

"Now don't clutch me or wiggle. I've got you safely if you'll only leave yourself to me."

Perhaps some half-instinctive memory of "rescue stunts" in the bay came to Dimsie's dazed brain, occasions when she had submitted to being "saved" for the benefit of the older girls. Obediently she relaxed all effort, and knew very little of what followed till she found herself in her own bed again at Jane's, with Matron doing something or other which seemed to make her very comfortable.

"Well, I lost the tub race," she observed drowsily, "and Mabs bet Winnie six chocolates – Oh, Matron, you'll never guess! Nita saved me!"

"Be quiet and go to sleep," said Matron, drawing the curtain. "I'll hear all about it afterwards."

It was past supper time when Dimsie woke again, feeling sleepy still, but much more like her usual self, to find Miss Yorke bending over her.

"Can I see Nita, please?" asked Dimsie promptly. "I'm under an – an obligation to her, and I'd like to thank her before I go to sleep again, which I might do at any minute."

"Very well," said Miss Yorke, smiling. "You eat this scrambled egg, and I'll send for Nita. Feeling better now?"

"Oh, yes, thank you!" responded Dimsie. "I'm not in the least ill, but I've been and lost Mabs six chocolates, though I did tell her not to be so certain of them. P'r'aps it's a judgement on her for betting – do you think so, Miss Yorke?"

Miss Yorke's mouth twitched oddly, as it often did in conversations with Dimsie.

"If she's lost her bet, that's a judgement that often falls on people," she said drily. "It won't hurt Mabs to do without her chocolates. Eat up your scrambled egg, Dimsie."

A few minutes later Miss Yorke slipped out of the room as Nita entered, rather sullenly, and stood beside Dimsie's bed.

"Feeling all right again?" she asked. "You look a bit pale."

"Oh, I'm all right, thanks," said Dimsie readily. "Really, Nita, I just wanted to tell you I'm ever so grateful to you for saving my life, and I'm sorry I cheeked you about Rosamund and the tennis club, but you see, it was the only thing to be done."

Nita's face relaxed suddenly.

"Your disagreeable duty, in fact?"

"Yes, but of course I can see that it must have been rather annoying for you, and therefore it was all the kinder of you to save my life this morning."

Nita gave a curious laugh.

"Don't mention it! I know all you kids think me a pretty miserable villain, but I could scarcely leave one of you to drown. Still, since I had to save somebody, Dimsie Maitland, strangely enough, I'm glad it was you."

Dimsie stared up at her with brown eyes of astonishment.

"But – but why? None of the others was ever as cheeky to you as me."

"Haven't a clue," responded Nita. "There's no accounting for tastes, you know, and though I don't think much of anybody in this precious establishment, on the whole, you're the least offensive. Now, you're supposed to be quiet and go to sleep, so goodnight."

And stooping down, she gave her an abrupt peck on the

cheek before leaving the room.

"Well!" exclaimed Dimsie, as she stared into the gathering shadows. "I never heard of anything so incredible!"

She was sound asleep when Miss Yorke returned later on to tuck her up for the night. The headmistress stood in silence, gazing down at the small flushed face, with its sweet, determined little mouth, and long dark lashes lying like shadows on the soft cheek below.

"None the worse," she whispered to Daphne, who had crept in behind her. "If it's true that character shows most strongly in a sleeping face, what a lot of it is there for eleven years old! Daphne, dear, your little cousin is going to be a credit to Jane's, a wonderful influence on the other girls. She is doing her bit already in the Lower School. I look forward to the day when she moves up further."

Daphne stooped down and lightly kissed the brown curls tossed across the pillow.

"She's a good little soul," she answered, with affectionate pride.

## THE END